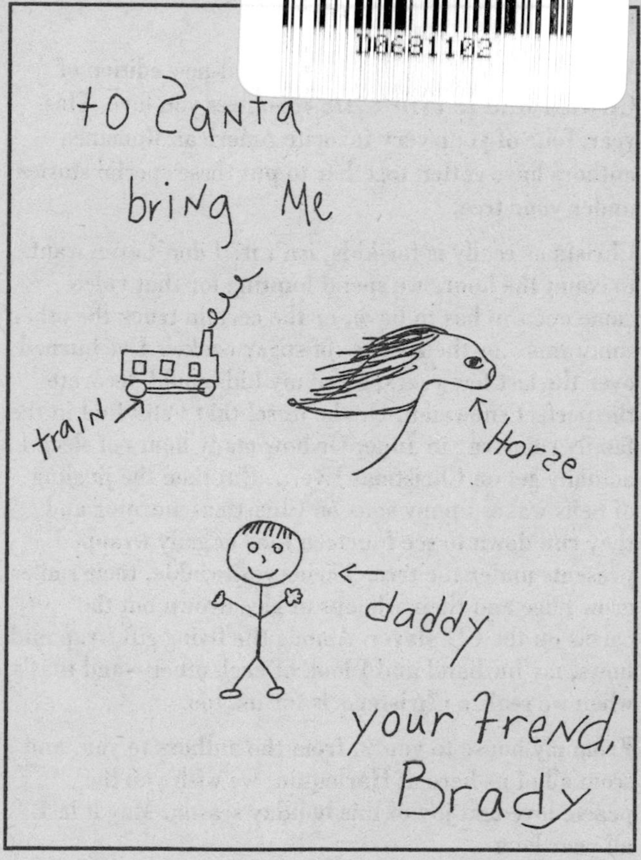
to Santa
bring Me
train
Horse
daddy
your frend,
Brady

Dear Reader,

We're delighted to bring you a brand-new edition of CHRISTMAS IS FOR KIDS romances you love. This year, four of your very favorite American Romance authors have gotten together to put these special stories under *your* tree.

Christmas really is for kids, isn't it? I don't even want to count the hours we spend hunting for that video game one son has to have, or the certain truck the other son wants...or the batches of sugar cookies I've burned over the last few years, all so my kids could decorate the perfect snowman. Or the tinsel that I still find in the family room rug in June. Or how many hours of sleep I actually get on Christmas Eve.... But then the jingling of bells wakes up my sons on Christmas morning and they run down to see fourteen tons of gaily wrapped presents under the tree. Their eyes twinkle, their smiles grow huge and their whoops of glee drown out the carols on the CD player. Among the flying gift wrap and bows, my husband and I look at each other—and that's when we realize Christmas is for us, too.

From my house to yours, from the authors to you, and from all of us here at Harlequin, we wish you the peace, love and joy of this holiday season. May it last all year long.

Debra Matteucci
Senior Editor and Editorial Coordinator
Harlequin Books
300 East 42nd Street

Cowboy Santa

JUDY CHRISTENBERRY

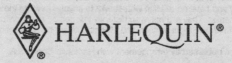

HARLEQUIN®

TORONTO • NEW YORK • LONDON
AMSTERDAM • PARIS • SYDNEY • HAMBURG
STOCKHOLM • ATHENS • TOKYO • MILAN • MADRID
PRAGUE • WARSAW • BUDAPEST • AUCKLAND

ISBN 0-373-16755-5

COWBOY SANTA

Chapter One

"Ho, ho, ho, little boy, what's your name?"

Sam Crawford eased the little guy onto his lap, smiling beneath his white beard. The kid didn't look at all nervous.

"Brady," the child said in a sturdy voice.

"Brady. That's a fine name. What's your last name?"

Sam, aka Santa, had never seen the child before, and he had to get all the information so the child's list could be sent to his parents. After all, each family was donating five dollars to charity for that very reason.

The little boy stared at Sam. "I thought Santa knew everything."

Sam shifted in his thronelike chair. "I know most things, but there are so many children to keep up with. It helps if you remind me."

"Oh. So you don't get me mixed up with other kids?"

"That's right."

"Brady Evans."

"Aha. Brady Evans. Good. Tell me, Brady, what do you want Santa to bring you for Christmas." While he was asking the standard question, he checked out the clock on the wall. Five more minutes and Kevin would be relieving him, taking his turn in the big red suit.

"A train," the little voice said determinedly, as if sure of his list.

He scanned the crowd, wondering which set of parents had produced this little guy. He was great.

"A train? Well, I'll see what I can do. Is there anything else you want?"

Sam noticed one woman watching the little boy closely. Ah, had to be his mother. And a very good-looking mother she was, too. Lucky daddy.

"A horse."

"A rocking horse?"

"No, a real one."

Sam raised his eyebrows. A horse was a little larger than a train, and more difficult to deliver. But in Wyoming, it wasn't unusual for a child to have his own horse. Though maybe not at four years of age, which was what he guessed his latest customer to be.

"Well, now, Brady, a horse is kind of big. Do you have room for one?"

"He can sleep with me." The little guy beamed up at him, as if he'd promised to deliver the animal.

"Uh, no, Brady, horses can't sleep with people. They need a stable, and a big pasture." Did his mother know what her son was asking for? Sam looked for the strawberry blonde he'd earlier spotted, but he couldn't find her.

"We have a big backyard," Brady assured him solemnly.

"Um, it might be better to start with a smaller animal, like a puppy. Have you talked to your parents about a puppy?"

"I want a horse," Brady said stubbornly, his little jaw clenched. Man, his parents were going to have a tough time when he got old enough to enforce that hardheadedness. Sam grinned. His own mother had complained often enough about him for the same reason.

"We'll see. I can't make any promises about a horse. They're kind of big to carry in my sleigh."

He couldn't keep from giving the child a hug, sort of a consolation for not promising him his Christmas wish.

"Well, now, you be a good little boy, and I'll see if I can find a few other—"

He stopped because Brady was tugging on his whiskers. He feared the child would soon expose him as a fraud. "Don't pull my beard, Brady. It hurts Santa."

"I'm not through."

"How old are you?" Sam demanded, checking the child out a little more closely. He seemed pretty self-possessed for such a little guy.

"Four," the boy said, holding up that many fingers.

"Okay. What else?"

"I want a daddy. He's not as big as a horse, is he?"

Joni Evans held her hand out to Brady, a big smile on her face.

Yes, she'd made the right decision. One day in town, and already things were better.

"Did you talk to Santa?" she asked her beloved child.

Brady nodded. "He said a horse can't sleep with me."

Joni's eyes rounded. "Wise Santa. Did you ask for a horse?"

"'Course I did, Mom. How can I be a cowboy without a horse?"

"You have a point, Brady, but I think we may have to wait a little while before we get a horse. You know, settle in, get to know our neighbors." Maybe even unpack first. They'd arrived in Saddle that morning, having had time only to drop their belongings at the house the school district had located for her.

"But, Mom, all the other kids will have horses," Brady complained, using the standard argument children employed anytime they wanted something.

"Uh, Mrs. Evans?"

Both Joni and Brady turned around, surprised. They'd only met the school superintendent, Mr. Brownlee, that morning. No one else in town knew them.

"Hi, Santa," Brady said, more enthusiastically

than when he'd first approached the man in the red suit. "Did I forget something?"

Joni tried to hide her smile when Santa appeared surprised by Brady's question. Before he could discover an answer, Brady had another question.

"Look! There's another Santa! How many Santas are there in Wyoming?"

Santa appeared even more panicked. "Uh, I'm supposed to— I have to— Mrs. Evans, I need to talk to you."

Had Brady said something wrong? Joni eyed her son even as she considered the Santa's words. "I'm going to show Brady some of the decorations. Why don't you look for us after you, um, change?"

Relief filled his gaze. "Right. I'll just be a few minutes."

He hurried away. She watched him leave, then turned to look at the new Santa. Not as big. Santa number one must tower over the elves. The new Santa's padding looked more believable, too.

"Do I need to talk to the other Santa, too?" Brady asked. "I want to be sure he knows what I want."

Joni had an answer at once. She didn't want to stand in line another half hour. "No. Remember, in Chicago, I told you all those Santas were the real Santa's helpers. It's the same way here. The first Santa will report what you wanted. Come over here. I think I see some gingerbread houses."

Brady scampered ahead of her in the direction she'd indicated. Joni took a deep breath. She'd worried she'd moved too fast for her four-year-old, taking this job suddenly, moving almost overnight, right before Christmas.

But it was as if a fresh breeze had blown through their lives. They'd shed the angst of Brady's grandparents and discovered a real Christmas spirit.

Thanksgiving at the Evanses had been tense and sad. Joni and Brady had left the next morning for Wyoming. They arrived this morning, Saturday, and discovered the town of Saddle had a Christmas party, with Santa, for the entire town.

They even had a spare Santa or two.

Joni smiled as she watched Brady exchange a rapid-fire conversation with the lady guarding the gingerbread houses from hungry fingers. What a relief to see him discard his silence.

Maybe she'd regret that later, she thought with a chuckle.

"Mrs. Evans?"

It was the same deep voice that had accosted her before. She turned with a smile in place. Then almost swallowed her tongue.

This was Santa? This big hunk? He wasn't much older than her, early thirties, probably. Not an ounce of fat on his muscular body, now encased in boots, jeans, a sheepskin-lined jacket and a cowboy hat.

"Santa?" she asked, her voice rising in disbelief.

When he grinned, she almost fainted, though she'd never done so in her life. If the women in Chicago knew what they were missing, they'd move en masse.

"Yes, ma'am. Temporary Santa." His blue eyes sparkled with the humor of his smile.

"Well," she said with a sigh, "I think you've ruined his image for me. I'll never be able to think of him as a round, jolly little man after this."

He seemed to enjoy her teasing. "I'll try to eat more."

"You do that," she said with a chuckle, figuring he ate a lot as it was to fill up his tall frame.

"Where's Brady?"

"Over there, looking at the gingerbread houses. Did he do something wrong?" She had visions of her son using an inappropriate word he'd heard at day care. Surely Santa had heard them before.

"No, he's a neat kid. And you'll get your letter. At least, that's why I want to talk to you."

"Oh, you need our new address? We just got here today, so I guess you wouldn't know it. We've moved into Mrs. Lindstrom's house on Sombrero Road. The number is—"

"You filled out the form before, remember?"

She laughed. So much had happened so quickly, it wasn't a surprise that she'd forgotten. "Oh, of course. Then—"

"Mom?" Brady interrupted. "If I can have a dollar, I can win a neat gingerbread house. Can I? Can I?"

"Yes, of course, sweetie. Excuse me a moment, Mr.—uh, I don't know your name." She dug into her purse and pulled out a dollar for her child.

"Hi," Brady said with a smile, showing no shyness.

"Hi, yourself. My name's Sam Crawford."

Brady stuck out his hand, man-style, which brought another smile to Joni's lips. "I'm Brady."

The man took his little hand and shook it with serious intent, as if Brady were as tall as him. "Glad to meet you. Welcome to Saddle."

Brady beamed at him, then said, "I'll be back in a minute."

After he dashed away, Joni looked at the handsome man. "You're great with kids. No wonder they let you be Santa."

"Let me? Lady, I was drafted," he protested, but he kept smiling.

"Now, what's the problem with Brady."

"Uh, I assume you're single?" he asked.

She stiffened. What did her marital status have to do with Brady's visit with Santa? Or was the man asking for personal reasons? That thought had her cheeks heating up. "Why do you want to know?"

He must have read her mind because he snapped, "Not for why you think! I mean, your son asked for a daddy for Christmas."

SAM COULD BELIEVE that a lot of men hit on Ms. Evans. She was a beauty, no doubt about that. But he wasn't one of them. 'Cause he'd just signed his final divorce papers last week. It wasn't like he was out looking.

No, *sirree*. He wasn't ready for that kind of mess again, if ever.

He took a step back as she drew a deep breath, pulling his gaze from an inappropriate part of her well-shaped anatomy. "Look, lady, I just thought you should know."

That defensiveness disappeared and she smiled at him, a real winner of a smile. "I'm so sorry. I didn't mean to be— I mean, we're new to town and— Anyway, no, I'm not married. Brady's daddy was a policeman in Chicago. He was killed a year ago last summer."

"I'm sorry," Sam said, his brows snapping together. She was altogether too young and beautiful to have such a tragic history.

"Thanks," she said, her smile still in place. "And thanks for the warning about Brady's request. I guess I'll have to—to head him off at the pass." Her smile widened and just the hint of a dimple appeared in her left cheek. "I'm trying to work on my Western vocabulary so I'll fit in."

The urge to place a kiss just where the dimple appeared surprised him. What was wrong with him? He'd sworn off women. Taking another step backward, he said, "I'm sure you'll fit in just fine, Mrs. Evans."

Tipping his hat to her, he turned away, only to be stopped by Brady's return.

"Mr. Crawford?"

"Yeah, Brady?"

"Do you got horses?"

He could feel her brown-eyed gaze on him, drawing him, filling him with a fierce need to escape. But he wasn't going to be rude to the little boy. "Yeah, Brady, I do. I live on a ranch."

Brady's eyes widened. "Wow! Could I see your horses?"

"Brady!" his mother said. "It's impolite to ask for an invitation."

Sam knelt down. He was a soft touch with children. He'd always wanted—expected—to have some of his own. Too bad that having children meant having a wife, too. "Tell you what, after you and your mom get settled in, maybe you can come out to the ranch and meet my nephew. He's four, too."

Brady was practically bouncing up and down. "Really? 'Cause I don't know any boys here. Thank you."

To Sam's surprise, he threw his arms around Sam's neck and squeezed tightly.

"Brady! You should thank Mr. Crawford, not attack him."

"I did, Mom!" Brady protested. "Didn't I?"

"You certainly did," Sam agreed with another smile. "Say, did you see the reindeer outside? When you leave, get your mom to take you by the corral."

"Okay. Come on, Mom," Brady insisted, taking her hand and tugging her toward the door.

The lady paused before following her son. "Thank you again, Mr. Crawford. You've been very gracious to a couple of strangers."

Sam nodded. The lady wouldn't be a stranger long in their little town. The bachelors would swarm around her like bees to honey. Brady would probably have his Christmas wish filled in no time.

But not by Sam.

"GOOD NIGHT, SWEETIE," Joni whispered, kissing her child just as he was nodding off. Sometimes it seemed that was the only time he stayed in one place long enough for her to hug him.

When she reached the hallway, she debated which chore to do next, now that Brady was down for the night. Their furniture was in place, thanks to the movers, but she had a lot of boxes to unpack.

With a sigh, she turned to the kitchen. Organizing the kitchen was the most important of their needs. She'd bought shelving paper that afternoon, before she'd called a halt to her work to take Brady to the Christmas party.

Again, she told herself she'd made the right decision. Last Christmas had been difficult. Her husband Derek's parents hadn't recovered from his loss. Brady deserved more than the misery they'd shared last year.

She'd expected Mr. and Mrs. Evans to gradually recover, but instead, Mrs. Evans seemed to grow worse. She was trying to make Brady into Derek.

Joni hadn't known what to do. Then, as if it were meant to be, she'd seen an ad asking for a teacher immediately...in Saddle, Wyoming.

In the middle of the semester?

She'd waited until her conference period the next day and called the number given. After that, a roller coaster of events brought her to this snug little house in a small town nestled at the foot of a mountain range. The town was named for the shape of a nearby peak in the Rocky Mountains, said to resemble a saddle.

What a change from Chicago.

But a good change. Brady had immediately taken to his new home. She laughed softly to herself as she remembered his asking her if he really could go outside whenever he wanted. Probably the freedom of having a yard had inspired the horse request.

And the daddy request?

She didn't think Brady remembered Derek. He'd been two when his daddy died. And Derek hadn't been much for babies. She'd loved her husband, but after Brady was born, they'd had a difficult time of it.

Maybe she wasn't cut out to be a wife. Just a mother. And she'd gotten lucky because her child was wonderful. And she'd do anything for him.

So here she was, feeling as if she'd taken a role in a Western movie, with every man wearing a cowboy hat and boots and drawling his words. And some of them, like Sam Crawford, looking like cowboy heroes come to life.

Enough of that! she told herself. She needed to get them settled in and make plans for Monday. Brady would go to a sitter that she planned to interview tomorrow, and she would start teaching a class of second-graders who had lost their teacher when her husband had taken a new job in California.

She didn't need to be thinking about a long, lean cowboy with a smile that could rev any woman's engine.

Even Mrs. Claus's.

SAM TUGGED AT HIS TIE before he'd even gotten out the door of the church the next morning. A lot of men in Saddle didn't bother with the blasted thing, but his mother would be horrified.

"Hey, Sam!" his friend Dustin called.

He turned around. The two of them had grown up in Saddle, attended school together, played sports and now worked their fathers' ranches. "Hey, Dusty, how's it going?"

"Great. Did you see the new lady in town?"

"You mean Mrs. Evans?" Who else could Dusty mean? They didn't have people moving to town all that often. And he'd seen her several rows away. Her hair was like a golden halo. Besides, Brady had waved to him.

"Don't know her name, but she's a beautiful blonde. Great curves, if you know what I mean. And a smile that lights up a room, with a little—"

"All right, already. I've seen her. What about it?" He didn't need all that detail thrown in his face again.

"Just thought you might be interested. I mean, after all, you're through with Linda, aren't you?"

"Off with the old, on with the new? You're moving a little fast for me, buddy."

"You can't waste time. You know she'll have her opportunities around here. Why, I heard three guys have already asked her out."

Sam let out a sigh of relief. She'd be hitched up with someone in no time. And he didn't prey on other people's property. "Good."

Dusty shrugged his shoulders. "Yeah, but how did you know she turned them all down?"

They had continued walking out to the parking lot, but now Sam came to an abrupt halt. "What?"

"You didn't know?"

"How do you know? What are you, the new gossip in town?" The woman had only been here two days. How could three men be after her already and already been rejected?

"She was at the town party last night. Mick Bowman cozied up to her right away. Everyone saw that. Except you 'cause you were playing Santa. She sent him away with his tail between his legs. Then Larry Cranston told me himself he asked her out to Sunday dinner today, but she said no. Didn't even say she'd take a rain check."

"Hell, she just moved in. They should give her time to breathe."

Dusty grinned. "We're starving for beautiful single women out here. If you wait too long, you won't even have a bone to gnaw on."

"If Lisa hears you talking like that, she's going to wonder if you still love her."

"Nope. She knows," Dusty assured him, a satisfied look on his face that brought pain to Sam. He'd thought, when he asked Linda to marry him, that he'd be satisfied, too.

"Well, I'm sure she'll settle into a social life soon."

Dusty wasn't about to be put off. "Don't you want to know who else she turned down?"

"There's more?"

Dusty held up three fingers and ticked off the two names he'd mentioned. Then he said, "The other one was the pastor."

Sam stared at his friend. The minister had moved there about six months ago. Everyone understood that he had a lady waiting for him in Kansas City. "I thought he was engaged?"

"Me, too, but if he is, he's not following his own advice. You know, about honesty and all."

"Yeah, I know." He looked back at the congregation standing in groups, chatting, even though the weather was cold. At least there wasn't a fierce wind. Unusual for the end of November.

"So, don't you think you should ask her?" Dusty said, nudging him with an elbow.

Had he missed some of Dusty's conversation? "Ask her what?"

"Man, is your brain frozen today? Ask her out on a date."

He wished other parts of him were frozen, because he didn't like the way his body responded to the sight of Joni Evans in a powder blue suit, the skirt short enough to show a great pair of legs.

"Nope. I don't think so."

But if she kept turning the men of Saddle down, he'd have to do something. To make sure he didn't let temptation overpower him.

He started mentally composing a list of men who could fulfill Brady's request for Christmas.

But he wouldn't put his own name on the list. Oh, no, not him.

Chapter Two

"You're not going to leave, too, are you?" one of her new students asked Joni as she accepted a hug goodbye at the end of her first week.

"No, of course not, Allison. I'll see you on Monday."

As if she hadn't answered, the little girl said, "'Cause Mrs. Miller told us goodbye on Friday and she didn't come back."

"I promise I'll be back on Monday. I like it here." And that was the truth. She hugged several other children and waved goodbye as they left her classroom.

Her first week had been remarkable. No hint of the violence that had seemed to surround her children in Chicago. No parents storming through her door with complaints.

The faculty was friendly, the parents grateful, and the children an absolute delight. The superintendent had told her that her class size would be small and supplies were no problem. She hadn't quite believed him. But the oil and coal-rich area had plenty of funds.

She sank back into her chair with a satisfied sigh. Brady was happy, too. He loved his day care, which was fortunate since it was about the only one in town. Every morning this week he'd been eager to leave the house.

"Ahem."

Joni spun around at the sound.

Standing in her doorway was Sam Crawford, the handsome Santa. He was holding a beautiful little girl about two years old. Beside him were two little boys.

One of them hers.

"Brady! What are you doing here? Is something wrong?" she demanded as she sprang from her chair to clutch her son to her breast.

"Nothing's wrong, Mrs. Evans," the man assured her calmly.

"Then why did Mrs. Barker let you take my son?" she demanded, shoving Brady behind her, as if to shield him.

He stared at her as if she'd lost her mind. "Because I told her I'd bring him to you. What's wrong with that?"

"Brady knows not to go with anyone but me," she said. Her voice was strong but it faltered as she reached the end of her words.

This wasn't Chicago.

"Do you—do you know Mrs. Barker?"

He nodded. "I guess so. She was my Sunday school teacher when I was five. My Cub Scout leader when I was seven. A chaperone on my senior trip. My—"

"All right." Joni interrupted, holding up a hand, feeling ridiculous. "I get the picture. I'm sorry, but in Chicago—"

"This isn't Chicago."

Well, she'd already told herself that. She couldn't blame him for saying the same thing.

"Of course." With a bright smile that covered her unease, she hoped, she nodded. "Thanks for bringing Brady."

"But, Mom," Brady protested. He'd at least realized she was dismissing the cowboy, even if Sam Crawford hadn't moved. "He asked me!"

She looked down at her child. "What, Brady?"

"He asked me to come play with Peter."

Peter. Her son had talked about Peter all week. A little boy who came every morning to Mrs. Barker's day care for half a day of classes. He and Brady had become friends, making Joni's life easier.

"How do you know—" she started asking Sam, but her gaze fell to the little boy standing beside him. "Is this Peter?"

"You haven't met him? He's at Mrs. Barker's every day."

"But only in the morning. I've been in a hurry this week in the mornings. I didn't go in and visit." She chewed on her bottom lip before she asked her next question. "Is—is Peter your son?"

"No. He and Katie here are my nephew and niece."

Drat! She hadn't wanted any connection with the

tall, handsome cowboy. He was too tempting for words, and she didn't want to be tempted.

"I'm glad to meet you, Peter. Brady really likes playing with you." She smiled at the little boy and he shyly smiled back.

"My sister's quite pleased, too. Peter is, uh, not outgoing, and she put him in child care so he could learn to socialize."

"I'm sure he's doing well," Joni said with an encouraging smile for the little boy. "Brady, why don't you and Peter go draw me a picture on the blackboard?"

Brady hadn't been in this schoolroom before, but he'd visited his mother's work in Chicago. He had no hesitation in leading the way. Peter followed in his footsteps.

Once the two boys were busy, she said softly to her guest, "Mr. Crawford, it's best not to talk about a child in front of him, as if he were invisible."

"I didn't mean—hell, I—" He came to an abrupt halt as he realized he'd committed another faux pas in front of children. Very carefully, he began again, "I just wanted you to know that my sister is pleased Brady is Peter's friend."

She ducked her head to hide her grin. Macho man didn't like her pointing out his error. But he'd handled it nicely. "Then it's mutual. I look forward to meeting her."

"Hey, Mom, look. Me and Peter drew some horses," Brady called.

Joni thought the horses in Wyoming must be quite

different from any she'd ever seen, or the two boys were not destined to be artists. "Terrific. Those are amazing horses. Can you erase them now? We need to go home, and the boards have to be clean before we go."

Instead of doing as she asked, Brady put down his chalk and raced back to her side. "No, Mom, I told you. He asked me."

"What are you talking about?"

"Uh, Mrs. Evans, the reason I picked up Brady, too, is that I thought he might spend the evening out at the ranch."

She stared at him, unprepared for the invitation.

"With Peter and Katie," he hurriedly added. "And me," he added again, when she still stared at him. "I usually baby-sit the pair of them on Friday nights so my sister and her husband have a little free time."

"That's very kind of you, Mr. Crawford," Joni began, "but I don't think—"

"Mommy, please!" Brady asked, an anxious look on his face.

She knew how much he wanted it because he called her Mommy. Normally she was Mom. But she was going to have to disappoint him. And things had been going so well. "Sweetie, we have a lot to do, and we're just getting to know everyone. I think it might be best if we put off your visit for a week or two."

Peter had returned to Sam Crawford's side, slipping his hand into his uncle's larger one. "Is she saying no?" he whispered, but everyone could hear his question. "I'll be really good," he added, staring at Joni anxiously.

Joni knelt down to his level. "Of course you would be," she assured him. "But," she began as Brady slid an arm around her neck, "we're new to town, and it makes me nervous for Brady to go off without me."

"Aw, Mom," Brady complained, but he leaned his head against hers.

"You could come play, too," Peter said, his gaze flying up to his uncle. "Couldn't she, Uncle Sam?"

Joni stood, swinging Brady to her hip, embarrassed by the turn of the conversation.

"Of course, you're welcome to come along, Mrs. Evans. But I should tell you that I live with my parents. My mother is quite good with children." Sam Crawford sounded as if the last thing in the world he wanted was for her to tag along.

"Perhaps another time," she told the two boys.

"We was going to have so much fun," Brady said, his mouth drooping. "Sam said we could have a wiener roast."

"You should call him Mr. Crawford, sweetie. And it's too cold outside for a wiener roast."

"I asked him to call me Sam, and we were going to have a wiener roast in the house," the cowboy said, correcting her, his voice stern, as if she'd offended him.

"And marshmallows," Peter added, a hopeful look in his gaze.

The little girl, silent until now, clapped her hands and repeated, "Marshmallows."

"I don't—"

"Mrs. Evans," Sam interrupted. "Come along with Brady, so the kids can have their fun. You can meet my mother and father, who, I promise, are upstanding members of our community. You don't have to let Brady out of your sight the entire time, and I'll bring the two of you back whenever you say."

"Please, Mommy, please?" Brady appealed one more time.

Joni didn't want to say yes. She didn't want to spend an entire evening anywhere near the handsome cowboy. Especially not date night in the U.S.A. But it meant a lot to Brady.

"I suppose we could put off our chores until tomorrow, if Mr. Crawford is sure I won't be a bother by inviting myself." She challenged him with a cool stare.

"Not at all. I think we have plenty of wieners. Shall we go?"

Both boys cheered and Brady wriggled to be put down. When Joni did so, he and Peter raced for the door.

"Brady?" she called.

"Yes, Mom?"

"You forgot to erase the blackboard."

The look of apprehension disappeared from his face, replaced by a big smile. He raced back to the blackboard, Peter right on his heels.

"It's not necessary for you to drive us," she said quietly. "Just give me directions, Mr. Crawford, and we'll stop by the house, so I can change, and then—"

"There aren't a lot of street signs out in the country, Mrs. Evans. I'd better drive you the first time. And I think you can quit being so formal. My name's Sam."

"Ah. I should be informal with you while you call me Mrs. Evans?" She'd noticed that he never relaxed around her.

"I don't know your first name," he replied.

Her cheeks rosied. "Sorry. I'm Joni," she said, wondering if she should offer her hand.

"We're through," Brady announced as he and Peter arrived at their sides unnoticed.

"Oh, good, sweetie. You and Peter did a good job." She looked back at Sam to find him watching her. "Do you mind following me to my house so I can change?" She didn't think her skirt and blouse were appropriate for a wiener roast.

Sam indicated his jeans. "We're definitely casual."

Great. All she needed was an invitation to stare at his strong, muscular legs. She snapped her gaze back to his face. "I promise it won't take me long to change."

"No problem. Ready, guys?"

The two little boys followed him out of the room, and Joni quickly gathered her things to join them. Brady asked to ride with Sam when they reached her car. She understood why when she saw his big truck. Brady loved trucks.

"Yes, but wear a seat belt."

She expected Sam to remind her that they weren't

in Chicago again, but he said nothing. At least some things were the same in Wyoming.

SAM ENTERTAINED HIS NIECE with a doll and the boys with questions about their day, until Joni Evans re-emerged from her house.

As she opened the door, he sucked in his breath.

"What's wrong, Sam? Did you hurt yourself?" Brady asked.

He reluctantly drew his gaze from Brady's mother and swallowed. "Uh, no, I just banged my knee on the door, that's all."

Sam's gaze returned to Joni. She was shrugging into a coat as she walked toward them, and Sam was glad. Anything to cover those delicious curves that could inspire a lot of fantasies.

She'd released her long blond hair from its earlier bondage, letting it fall on her shoulders. And the tight jeans and waist-length lilac sweater that clung to her curves, now covered by her coat, didn't remind Sam of any schoolteacher he ever had.

"Yea! Mom brought some cookies. She makes good cookies," Brady assured his friend as Joni opened the door.

"What kind of cookies?" Peter asked.

Joni smiled at him as she slid into the front seat next to Katie's car seat. "Oatmeal raisin. Do you like them?"

While Peter was giving her enthusiastic approval, she looked at Sam. "I thought they would be a good snack for the children."

"That's thoughtful of you, but not necessary. We do have food at our house." He was being difficult, he knew, but somehow she rubbed him the wrong way. Wrong verb! he quickly cautioned himself. He was going to avoid touching her in any fashion.

She stiffened beside him.

"Sorry, I didn't mean to sound— The cookies are fine. In fact, I'd like one right now." He couldn't think of any other way to apologize.

Her eyebrows shot up. "You don't mind the children eating one now, too?"

"Of course not."

She unwrapped the plate of cookies and offered him one. "Sorry. My husband never wanted Brady to eat anything in the car."

She served the boys each a cookie, then asked about Katie.

"If you don't give her one, you'll hear her scream from here to Casper," he assured her. "Katie is no shrinking violet."

"Good," Joni said with a smile as she held out a cookie for the little girl.

"Cookie!" Katie crowed with excitement, holding it up to Sam. He pretended to bite her cookie and she jerked it back to her chest, squealing.

Everyone laughed at Katie's antics, and some of the tension left the cab of the truck. As he took a bite of his cookie, Sam put the truck into gear and backed out of their driveway. "Hey, these are good."

"I told you," Brady said from the jump seat.

Sam grinned at Joni, then turned his attention to the driving. It was safer.

"How far do you live from town?"

"Not that far. About ten miles. My great-grandfather built the house on the corner of our property closest to town."

"So your family has been here a long time."

"Yeah. Is your family still in Chicago?"

"I don't have any family. My husband's parents are there, along with his two brothers and their families."

He frowned. It must be tough to be alone, but she didn't show any stress about it. "Will you go visit them for Christmas?"

He noted that Joni checked to see if Brady was listening before she answered. The two boys were whispering and giggling. "No, I don't think so. We've just gotten settled in here. Maybe we'll visit them next summer."

"So you're planning to stay?"

"Oh, yes. So far it's been great."

"Cold weather doesn't bother you?"

She chuckled, a husky sound that made him think of warm, thick honey. "I'm from Chicago, Sam, not Florida. It's not exactly balmy. We're known as the Windy City, remember?"

"Then you'll fit right in here. Most of our snow comes sideways because of the wind." When she returned his smile, he hurriedly looked away.

"Cookie!" Katie squealed.

They both laughed as the little girl beamed at them, cookie crumbs and drool all over her face.

Joni pulled a tissue from her purse and twisted around to clean her face.

"Cookie!" Katie demanded again.

"Me, too," the boys called.

"Sorry," Joni said. "They're for dessert, after dinner."

Though the boys grumbled, they agreed to wait. Sam liked the way she handled the four-year-olds. Katie, of course, was another matter.

"Cookie!" she continued to shriek.

"Oh, sweetie, your tummy is so little, I'm afraid your mommy would be unhappy if I gave you another one. How old are you? Are you two?" She held up two fingers.

Distracted, Katie reached for the fingers.

"She's two. Marty calls them the terrible twos."

"I remember them," Joni agreed with a smile, but Sam thought her gaze held a hint of sadness.

"Was Brady a handful?"

Her smile broadened again. "Always."

He could believe it. Her son was the opposite of shy Peter. Although his nephew had been more exuberant today, in Brady's company, than he could remember.

They turned onto the gravel road that would carry them to the ranch, making the ride a little rougher. "Glad you didn't bring your car?" he asked.

"Frankly, yes, but I hate for you to drive us back later."

"No problem. Peter and Katie will spend the night, but once they're in bed, it won't take long to bring you back."

"Your mother will watch them while you're gone?"

"Of course," he answered indignantly. "I know better than to leave two little ones alone. I'm a good sitter, aren't I, Peter?"

"Yeah, Uncle Sam. You're the best."

Sam grinned triumphantly at Joni, as if he'd proved his worthiness.

"All you'd have to do to get a four-year-old boy's approval is feed him cookies," she suggested, teasing him.

He stared at those warm brown eyes, the elusive dimple that appeared, and he couldn't help smiling back. Then he caught himself as he almost drove off the road.

Man! The woman was dangerous. Or it had been too long since he'd been with a woman. Hell, he knew that was true. He and Linda had been separated the past six months prior to the divorce, and things hadn't been too good before that.

He cleared his throat. "Uh, there's the ranch house."

Pride filled him as he stared at the house he'd been born and raised in. Last New Year's, he'd promised Linda he'd build her her own house. He'd started it once the snow had melted, not far from his parents' house, but it stood half-finished. He'd lost heart when it became clear Linda wasn't staying.

His parents' house was a sprawling two-story, with lots of room for a big family. His father had wanted lots of kids, but his mother had miscarried her third child and the doctor had warned them not to try again.

When his sister Martha, or Marty as they called her, had married Paul Kessler, she'd moved into town. Paul was the only lawyer in Saddle and kept offices in the downstairs of their house.

Then Sam had proposed to Linda. He hadn't seen the need to build a separate house a few feet from his parents'. There was plenty of room for four people. But Linda hadn't seen it that way.

"Are they building a new house?" Joni asked.

He should have known she'd ask. "No."

She looked at him when he offered no other explanation, but he wasn't going to say anything else.

When he pulled the truck to a stop, the two boys jumped out, Peter anxious to introduce his friend to his grandparents.

For the first time, Joni seemed nervous. "Are you sure your mother won't mind that I came with you?"

"Nope. She likes to have company. You two will get on like a house afire." Strange. He didn't know why he was so sure of that fact. Linda and his mother had had little in common.

He took Katie out of the car seat. "Come on in. And don't forget those cookies, or the boys will revolt."

She sent him a grateful smile that had his pulse racing again. He'd better start concentrating on the kids.

"Mom? You home?" he called as he pulled open the back door and motioned for Joni to precede him.

"Of course I am. I've just met— Well, hello," his mother, Loretta, said with a smile when her gaze fell on Joni. "I didn't know we were having company."

Sam hastily made the introductions.

"I hope you don't mind. It's just that we only moved in last weekend and—and I don't know Sam that well, so I was nervous about letting Brady—"

"Land's sake, child, you don't have to explain to me. Better safe than sorry. Come right in. You're welcome here anytime."

"Thank you so much, Mrs. Crawford," Joni said, and Sam could see the earlier tension fading. "Everyone here has been so friendly."

"Yeah, I heard the men are after you already," his mother returned with a chuckle. "You should know that we have a great gossip chain around here. It's our entertainment, and you certainly have kept us entertained."

Joni's cheeks turned bright pink, which only made her more attractive.

Sam interrupted. "I told Joni she could join us for hot dogs tonight. We have plenty, don't we?"

"Sure. I bought everything you asked for," Loretta assured him.

"And I brought cookies for dessert," Joni said, holding out the plate.

"Cookie!" Katie squealed, once more reminded of what she wanted.

"Oops, sorry," Joni apologized to Sam.

"No problem. Come on, Katie, let's go find Grandpa."

As he started out the door, his mother called, "He's upstairs in the shower."

Sam paused, turning to stare at his mother. "Why?"

"We're going out this evening. You don't need us to help you with the kids, and Mabel and Ed asked us over to play forty-two. That's okay, isn't it?"

Sam stared at Joni, his mind awhirl. He was going to be left alone with Joni? But he'd planned on his parents being there, to chaperone.

Joni, as well as his mother, was staring at him. When she licked her lips, he almost groaned.

"If it's not, perhaps your parents could give us a lift back into town."

"Nonsense," Loretta said, a mischievous grin on her face. "Sam will be glad of the company. He's been alone too much lately."

Uh-oh. His mother was matchmaking.

Just what he didn't need.

Chapter Three

Joni noticed the sudden tension between mother and son. "Please, if it's any trouble, we—" She didn't know what. After all, she didn't have a car.

"Don't be silly. Let me show you where everything is for the hot dogs while Sam entertains Katie," Loretta said, still staring down her son.

"Be careful, Mom," he said, warning his mother of something, but Joni wasn't sure what.

Once the door had closed behind him, Loretta showed Joni all the fixings she'd prepared. "I hear you're a widow," she chatted. "So young. What a shame. How did your husband die?"

"He was killed on duty as a Chicago cop."

Loretta straightened, her gaze filled with sympathy. "How sad."

Joni wasn't still mourning her husband. Nor her marriage, except as it had been that first year. She'd thought they would always be that happy. She smiled at Loretta. "It's been a while."

"Good. You're getting rave reviews from the parents already. They say you're very gentle with the little ones.''

"They're all adorable.''

"Even Jeremy Leghorn?'' Loretta asked with a knowing look.

Jeremy was a second-grader but he was built like a boy years older, already towering over everyone. And he was a firm believer in "might is right.''

"Jeremy keeps life from getting boring,'' Joni assured her hostess with a laugh.

"My, what a pretty smile,'' Loretta said, surprising Joni.

"Thank you. What will Katie eat?''

Thankfully her question sidetracked Loretta from any more personal comments for several minutes. Then she invited Joni to sit at the kitchen table and enjoy a cup of tea while they waited for the others' return.

"I just want to tell you I'm grateful you came along tonight.''

Joni raised her eyebrows. "You don't trust Sam with the children?''

"Oh, it's not that. He's a great baby-sitter. But I worry about leaving him alone right now.''

Joni didn't waste breath replying. She knew Loretta would tell her.

"You see, he signed his divorce papers last week and, well, I worry about him. You know how mothers are.''

"Last week? He seems quite composed for— I

mean, he doesn't seem to be—'' Joni wished she'd said nothing.

"Oh, he hides his emotions well. And the marriage was truly over much sooner. But it's hard, even so."

"Yes, I'm sure. Well, I'll help with the children."

"Just protect my kitchen. That boy is helpless in here. I guess I've spoilt him. As capable as he is—he's wonderful running the ranch—he can't seem to keep a kitchen clean."

"I'll do my best," Joni assured her just as the door opened and all three kids, Sam and a man she assumed was his father came through the door.

The older man spoke first. "Howdy, Brady's mom. Your son is sure a talker," the man, a handsome older version of his son, said.

"I'm afraid so, Mr. Crawford. You'll have to tell him when you need some peace." She stood as she spoke and extended her hand. "I'm Joni Evans."

"Well, no wonder my son brought you home," the man said as he shook her hand, a smile on his weathered face.

"Dad!" Sam protested.

"Actually I invited myself because I'm an overprotective mom. You can't blame Sam for that, Mr. Crawford."

"Uh-uh," he said with a grin directed toward Sam. "And make it Tom."

"I will, Tom. You and Loretta are being so friendly. I really appreciate that."

"We're glad to see a new face. You ready, Mother? Are we still going?"

"Of course we are. You know how Mabel loves her forty-two. Besides, now that Joni is here, we don't have to worry about Sam."

"Mother, she is not baby-sitting me!"

"Of course not, dear," Loretta said blandly and kissed both her grandchildren and added a kiss for Brady.

The lady won Joni's heart in that instant, making Brady feel a part of the family. Tom followed suit with hugs all around.

When the door closed behind them, Sam was still glowering.

Joni tried to hide her smile. "Do we eat now, or is there something else on the agenda?"

"I was going to play Candyland with the boys, but I don't know if we can keep Katie from eating the cards. We're already missing two."

"Let me play with Katie while you entertain the boys. I've missed having a baby around since Brady has grown so much." She reached out her arms and hugged the little girl as she came to her. "Ooh, you smell so good, Katie. Your mommy must've given you a bath just before your uncle came to get you."

"Yeah," Sam said with a nod. "That's where I draw the line. It's bad enough with Pete, here. He splashes me, but she's a maniac in the bathtub."

They all trooped into the family room and Joni fell in love with it at once. It was huge but cozy. A massive rock fireplace dominated the room, with plump sofas around it. In another area, a game table, with a lamp over it, invited one to indulge in games and puzzles. There were several other easy chairs with reading lamps, and a big-screen television.

Best of all, one wall was a huge picture window that looked out on the snowcapped Rockies. She would never tire of that scene.

"How beautiful," she murmured, her gaze traveling around the room.

"Yeah. Mom's doing."

"Is this where we're going to roast the wieners?" Brady asked, standing in front of the fireplace.

"Oh, no, dear," Joni said at once, sure that such a messy undertaking would be banished to the kitchen.

"Of course it is," Sam contradicted. He looked at Joni. "Don't worry. Mom says everything in here is washable."

Joni hoped so.

Sam led the two boys to the game table where Candyland awaited them.

Joni stared after him. He was every woman's dream—strong, intelligent, sexy and he was going to spend Friday night with three children, none of them his own.

"How long have you been doing this?" she asked before she thought about what his mother had told her.

"Doing what? Playing Candyland?" he asked, looking over his shoulder.

"No, of course not. Taking care of Peter and Katie."

"Off and on since Peter was born. I like kids."

She wondered if that had been the reason for his marriage breakup. But it was none of her business.

"Does Katie have some toys?" she asked, hoping to distract herself from such thoughts.

"Ask her," he suggested with a wry grin.

Katie was delighted to show Joni her box in one corner, crammed with toys. She introduced Joni to every item in the box, stopping to play with her favorites and inviting Joni to do the same.

An hour later, Sam suggested they have dinner.

"Bored to tears yet?" he asked under his breath as everyone headed for the kitchen.

She stared at him, surprised. "Of course not. I was thinking I wish I had a little girl, too. Boys are fun, but they don't want to play with dolls."

"Eeew! Yuck!" Brady said as he passed by her. "I would never play with dolls."

"Me, neither!" Peter seconded, but Joni noticed he gave his uncle a quick look, as if to be sure he didn't rat on him.

"Who's hungry?" Joni asked to change the subject. She didn't want Peter embarrassed. "How many hot dogs will we need?"

"Better bring the whole package," Sam suggested. "Here's a tray. If you'll gather all the ingredients, we'll spread out an old blanket in front of the fire and put on some more wood." Sam led the two boys out to the porch.

"Well, as usual, Katie, it looks like the women get to do the cooking."

"Me help," Katie assured her. Joni gave her some spoons to carry to the table.

When Sam came back in with the boys, he wore a frown.

"Everything okay?" she asked.

"Yeah, sure."

She didn't think so, but he obviously didn't want to say anything in front of the children. She grabbed the loaded tray, called to Katie and went into the den.

They settled on the blanket on the floor in front of the fireplace, and she helped the boys put their wieners on roasting forks and kept Katie out of everything until Sam could fix her a plate. She almost forgot Sam's preoccupation.

Once the children were eating, the two adults cooked their own wieners. In a low voice, she asked again, "What's wrong?"

He seemed surprised by her question. "Nothing, really. I mean, I knew we were supposed to get a snowstorm in a day or two, but it looks like it got here early."

"It's snowing? We'd better eat in a hurry so you can take us home right away," she said, pulling her wiener from the fire.

"Joni, I can't leave the kids here with my parents gone. And I don't like to take them out in bad weather unless I have to." He shrugged his shoulders. "It's not like you're in any danger here."

"You mean we have to spend the night?" she asked, her voice rising.

"Shh! No, of course not. As soon as my parents

get back, I'll take you home. They don't stay out late, especially if the weather gets bad.''

She fixed her plate, but she was still uneasy about their situation. When the wind rattled the window-panes with a particularly gusty blow, she jumped.

Katie whimpered and the two boys looked alarmed, but Sam assured them it was a snowstorm. Instead of being concerned, like all little boys, they cheered and raced to the window. Katie crawled over into her uncle's lap and snuggled against him.

Joni found herself almost envious of the child before she realized what she was thinking. But it had been so long since strong arms had held and comforted her. And Sam Crawford's arms appeared particularly inviting.

She looked up to discover him staring at her. With an awkward grin, she got to her feet. ''I'd better start putting everything away. I promised your mother I'd leave her kitchen clean.''

''I'll help,'' he said, starting to get up.

''No, keep an eye on the kids. I'll take care of the dishes.'' It would give her time to escape the powerful pull she felt toward the man. He had to have some flaws. No one could be as perfect as he appeared to be.

Half an hour later he came into the kitchen. ''How's it going in here? Are you about finished?''

''Yes, actually. How are the kids?'' They'd been amazingly quiet the past few minutes.

''All tucked up, waiting for a good-night kiss.''

She stared at him. ''Where's Brady?''

"I just told you, all tucked up—"

"Wait a minute. Brady's not sleeping here," she protested.

"Maybe not, but what's the point in keeping him awake until we leave? He might as well—"

"Don't you think you should've asked me before you made that decision for my child?" Maybe she was overreacting. But her husband had been a dictator when he was around, which, fortunately after Brady was born, wasn't often. But her in-laws had also wanted to make all her decisions.

She wouldn't tolerate it from them, so she sure wouldn't tolerate it from a relative stranger.

"Hey, settle down, Joni. You want him out of bed, march right up those stairs and ruin the best fun he and Peter have had in a while. Play the role of the wicked witch. I don't mind."

She couldn't believe he would blame the situation on her. "It wouldn't be my fault if they got upset. It would be yours for making a decision you had no right to make!"

The arrogant man just cocked his hands on his hips and raised one eyebrow. She drove past him, so angry she felt like taking a bite out of him.

By the time she reached the top of the stairs, she'd calmed down somewhat. "Brady?" she called softly.

"In here, Mom. Isn't this neat? Peter and I are having a sleep-over. I've never had one before."

By the time she reached the door of the bedroom, she knew she wasn't going to take her son back downstairs. But she had to warn him that he'd probably be in his bed in the morning. "Hi, sweetie, Peter. Are you both comfortable?"

The two boys giggled and assured her they were "snug as two bugs in a rug." "That's what Uncle Sam says," Peter added.

"I see." She tried to smile at the mention of the irritating man downstairs. She really did.

So neither of them would be upset if they each awoke alone, she said, "If Brady is gone when you wake in the morning, Peter, it will be because your uncle Sam took us home. We need to leave when your grandparents get back. But we'll plan a sleep-over at our house real soon, if this one gets cut short. Okay, guys?"

"Sam said it's okay, Mom. I don't take up much space," Brady assured her with a confident smile. It seemed Sam had taken on hero status sometime during the evening.

"Well, we'll see. At least you're all warm and comfy for now. And I've come to collect two goodnight kisses," she said, stooping over each little boy.

After she stepped out into the hallway, pulling the door closed behind her, she heard the soft music of a child's toy and opened the door across the hall to discover Katie already asleep in a white crib.

She might be angry with Sam Crawford, but she'd have to admit he was efficient. She hadn't gotten Brady to bed that fast in a long time.

Sam was standing at the bottom of the stairs, waiting for her. "What, no Brady kicking and screaming at being dragged out of bed?"

She marched stiffly past him into the den. "I had no intention of being cruel. But I don't like other people making decisions about my child."

He followed her. "I don't think putting a child to bed is something that needs a lot of discussion. He was as tired as Peter. They'd had a busy day."

She ignored him and ostentatiously checked her watch. "How long do you think your parents will be?"

"They should be back by ten."

An hour and a half alone with him? She nibbled on her bottom lip, as she did whenever she was thinking. Suddenly he was beside her and his thumb brushed across her mouth.

"Don't do that."

She jerked her head back. "What are you doing?"

"You don't understand how tempting it is for me to do the same thing."

When she stared at him, not understanding what he meant, he added, "Nibble on your lips."

She gasped and backed up.

He turned away, as if everything were normal, but Joni's heart was beating a rapid tattoo in her chest.

"Want to watch some television? We have a satellite dish, though we may not get good reception in the snowstorm."

"Is it getting worse?" she asked, moving to the windows and pulling the curtain aside. "Oh, my."

There was an outside light on the porch, but it was barely visible. The snow was blowing, as Sam had predicted, but it was thick and heavy.

"Yeah. I hope my parents get back okay."

"Will they even try?" she asked, her stomach sinking.

"Yeah. It's not as bad as it looks, if you know the roads. And Mabel and Ed are our closest neighbors." He stepped back from the window, giving her a little more room to breathe.

Then he added, "So, are you up to TV?"

A picture of the two of them on one of the sofas, snuggled together watching a movie, was completely unacceptable. She shook her head.

"I don't suppose you play chess?" Before she could even answer, he continued, "Most women don't, though I don't know why. It's a wonderful—"

"I'd love to play chess," she said, interrupting him. At least, that way she knew there would be a table between them.

AN HOUR LATER, when they barely heard the sound of a car over the noise of the wind, Joni was much happier. Concentrating on the chess game had helped her ignore the potent attraction of the man across from her.

Besides, though she'd lost the first game, it had been a close match. She'd seen a measure of respect appear in Sam's eyes that she'd enjoyed.

"Must be my parents," he said as he moved one of his pawns, then stood. "I'll go see if they need any help."

"I'll come with you."

She followed him into the kitchen, thinking about

their time together and almost regretting its end. She hadn't had much adult company in a while. By her choice, of course. Several of her husband's colleagues had invited her out, but she wanted nothing to do with another policeman.

Tonight, she and Sam had started out as adversaries, wary of each other, but their chess game had lessened their antagonism, somewhat.

When Sam swung open the door, a blast of cold wind and driven snow came inside with two bundled figures. Joni wrapped her arms around herself and shivered.

"My, my, my," Loretta said as she pushed the hood of her coat back. "That is some storm. We just barely made it. Everything all right here?"

"Yes, of course," Sam said.

"Shall I put on some water to heat? To make a cup of tea or coffee?" Joni suggested.

"Good idea, Joni," Tom agreed. "I feel half frozen. The truck didn't heat up much before we got here."

She filled the teakettle and got out two mugs.

"I'll take one, too, Joni, and you might as well join us," Sam suggested.

Joni couldn't expect Sam to go out in the storm without fortifying himself, and she wouldn't mind a cup of hot tea as well. She did as he asked, even if his words had sounded more like an order than a suggestion.

"I thought maybe you'd start home a little earlier," Sam said.

"Would've been back sooner if we'd realized how bad the storm was. But you know your mother and Mabel. They were whooping and hollering so loud 'cause they were beating us men that we couldn't even hear the storm."

Loretta grinned as she settled in at the kitchen table. "Your father hates losing," she said primly. "He always exaggerates because of that."

Joni enjoyed her hostess's smugness. "Do you two ever play as partners?"

Tom's only response was "Ha!"

"We have a few times, but he doesn't like the way I play, and I don't like him telling me how to play. We find it works much better if we play against each other," Loretta said with pleasure.

The water started boiling and Joni waved Loretta back into her seat. "I'll bring it all to the table."

"Thanks." Loretta settled back down. "I'm still half-frozen."

Joni loaded the tray she'd used earlier, adding what was left of the oatmeal raisin cookies.

"Cookies? I didn't know you had time to bake, 'Retta," Tom said.

"I didn't. Joni made them."

He bit into one, then smiled at Joni. "You're welcome here anytime, young lady, as long as you come with a plateful of cookies."

While Sam and Loretta protested his saying Joni wouldn't be welcome without cookies, Joni smiled at his teasing. "Thank you, Tom. I'll remember that."

They chatted a little longer, but Joni was becoming

anxious for them to be on their way. "I don't want to rush you, Sam, but shouldn't we get started before the storm gets too much worse?"

The other three stared at her. Finally Loretta said, "Oh, dear, Joni, the storm was bad enough just coming from Ed and Mabel's. Sam would never make it all the way to town and back. You'll have to spend the night."

Chapter Four

Sam watched Joni as she took in his mother's words.

"But I can't—we can't—spend the night. I don't have any clothes or— Your truck is very big," she added, turning to Sam.

Tom spoke before Sam could. "I almost went off the road several times. And the storm seems to be getting worse."

"I'll find some things for you to wear," Loretta said. "And there's plenty of food. We'll be fine."

"I—thank you. I'm sorry to be such a burden," Joni returned, then glared at Sam.

What had he done?

He'd kept his damn hands off her all evening. That in itself qualified him as a saint. Because she was mighty tempting.

"Oh! I just remembered!" Loretta said with a laugh.

Sam looked at his mother warily. She was enjoying their predicament just a little too much.

"Remember that white elephant Christmas party last year?" She beamed at all of them. "My present was those red bikini panties. I bet they'll fit you just perfect.''

With a suppressed groan, Sam leaped up from the table. He could remember those panties just fine. And now he'd picture them on Joni all night. Fat chance he was going to get any sleep. "I'll head on up to bed," he muttered.

"Before you do, son, dig out that terry-cloth robe Marty and Paul gave you last year. And a T-shirt for Joni, along with a pair of socks."

"Oh, no, I couldn't—" Joni protested.

"Won't hurt nothin'," Tom assured her. "That boy hasn't never worn a robe. It's been hanging in his closet since the day he got it."

Sam looked at his parents and shook his head. They were working this storm thing too hard. Yep, they were definitely matchmaking. What was wrong with them? He'd just gotten out of a disastrous marriage a week ago. They were already pushing him down the aisle again?

Well, they could forget it.

He stood. "Come on, I'll find those things for you."

With an uncertain look at his parents, Joni rose and followed him from the room.

Neither spoke on the way upstairs. When they reached his room, however, he closed the door behind them.

"I just want to make something clear," he growled, not bothering with the niceties.

"Yes?"

"I'm not looking."

She stared at him, blinking several times. Then, with a frown, she said, "I beg your pardon?"

Was she dense? Anyone could see what his parents were doing. "No matter what my parents tell you, I'm not looking for a wife." He glared at her to emphasize his words. Some women were hard to discourage.

He saw realization dawn in her eyes. Then anger. "Thanks for the warning. Maybe now I won't go into a decline when you ignore me." The saccharine sweetness of her words had him arching one brow.

"Just wanted you to know."

"Do you give every woman this warning, or am I special?"

She was still angry. Good. "Aren't that many women around here. And my divorce was recent. No way am I going to fall into that trap again."

"Trap? And you think only men feel trapped in marriage?" She put her hands on her hips and glared back.

His gaze traveled up and down her taut body, from her breasts, covered in a lilac sweater, to her hips, outlined faithfully in tight jeans. "It's the woman who always wants a ring. If you're interested in something else, just say so. I don't object to you sharing my bed...but not my life."

"No, thank you!"

She turned to leave.

"Wait. I've got to give you those things, or my

mother will be wanting to know why. I don't want to explain. Do you?"

She shook her head and stood stiffly at attention.

He shouldn't ever have mentioned her sleeping in his bed. Between that thought and the bikini panties, he might not sleep for a year or two.

He dug through the hangers until he found the white robe in the back. Of course, it would be white. He tossed it to Joni as he strode over to his chest of drawers. Whipping out a neatly folded T-shirt and a thick pair of white socks, he carried them to her. "That's everything."

With a nod, she turned and opened the door.

Unfortunately his mother was standing there.

"Oh, I thought maybe Sam had already shown you the guest room." She eyed the two of them speculatively, and Joni's cheeks burned.

"It took a while to find the robe," he muttered.

"Of course. Which proves he never wears it," Loretta said with a smile directed at Joni. "Your room is right next door to Sam's. And you'll share this bath, across the hall."

"Thank you," Joni said softly, ignoring Sam completely.

"There's plenty of towels if you want a shower tonight. Sam will be a gentleman and let you go first, won't you, son?"

"Yeah." Visions of sharing a shower with Joni came unbidden to his mind. Great. He was going to lose his mind.

"Then, if Sam doesn't mind, I think I will go first.

Thank you again for all your hospitality, Loretta,'' Joni said as she edged toward the bathroom.

''Wait, don't forget these,'' Loretta laughed as she dangled the red bikini panties in front of both of them.

Sam closed his eyes, wishing he could blot out his mind as easily. He didn't open them until he heard the bathroom door close.

''Mom,'' he muttered softly. ''I'm not interested.''

With a saucy smile, she whispered, ''Doesn't look that way to me.''

''She's a beautiful woman, and I am alive, but I'm not going to marry again. So forget whatever plans you've made.''

His father hit the top of the stairs in time to hear his words. He held up one hand, as if warding off evil. ''I didn't hear a thing.''

''Dad, tell her to butt out.''

''Not me. This is between you and your mother. Besides, I like Joni.''

Sam wanted to explode. ''That's not the problem!''

''Shh!'' Loretta warned. ''She'll hear you. And so will the babies.''

He couldn't take any more. He spun on his heel and went into his bedroom, closing the door behind him. Now he had to wait for Joni to finish taking a shower in his bathroom, and put on his T-shirt, his socks and those blasted red bikini panties.

It was going to be a long night.

WHEN JONI WOKE the next morning, she stretched under the covers, feeling reluctant to get out of bed.

Today was Saturday. She had a lot of chores to— She wasn't at home!

With a flash, last night's events came to mind. She'd spent the night at the Crawford ranch.

That thought had her rushing to the window. The storm had ended, but everything was white. Thankfully the snow didn't appear too deep, but a fierce wind kept blowing it across the land.

She spun around and reached for the terry-cloth robe Sam had loaned her. As she shrugged it on, she discovered a pile of clothing in the chair by the door.

A quick check confirmed what she'd suspected. Those were the clothes she'd worn yesterday—now freshly laundered and neatly folded. Loretta must have been up early. Joni checked her watch, only to discover it was already 9:40.

She stared at it. She couldn't possibly have slept that late. Always, she was up by seven.

But then she didn't usually lie awake half the night thinking about a man. An irritating, arrogant, handsome man. Sam Crawford had probably fueled many a woman's dreams.

But she wasn't going to let him fill hers, ever again. After all, he was bossy, and he wasn't interested. Two definite strikes against him.

She slipped into her sweater and jeans before carefully making her bed. Then she gathered the T-shirt, socks and underwear to take to Loretta's laundry room. The robe she left hanging across the back of a chair.

Downstairs, she found Loretta in the kitchen.

"Loretta, thanks so much for washing my clothes. I didn't even need to borrow the robe since I slept so late."

"I'm glad you slept well. And there was nothing to get up early for," the older woman said with a smile. "Sam won't be back to take you home until lunchtime. He and Tom went out to check on the stock."

"Oh. Well, I'm glad I didn't keep anyone waiting. Where are the kids?"

"In the den drawing. We've already made a snowman. Even Katie helped."

"My goodness, you've been busy. Can I do anything to help?" She felt like such a slacker.

"Well, you might check on the kids. I'm putting together a stew for lunch," Loretta explained with a smile.

Joni headed to the den. The boys were industriously drawing pictures at the game table, while Katie was once again going through her toy box.

"Good morning, guys," she said, greeting each with a kiss. "How are you this morning?"

Both boys showed her their numerous drawings, and Katie brought over a baby doll. She spent the rest of the morning with the children, though her gaze strayed occasionally to the window as she worried about a certain stubborn man out in the cold.

LORETTA WAS IN THE BARN doing some of their chores when Tom and Sam got back in.

"What are you doing out here?" Tom roared. "You'll freeze to death."

"Nonsense. It's not that cold in the barn," she said calmly, cleaning out a stall where they were keeping watch on a sick mare.

"But what about the kids?" Sam demanded.

"They're doing just fine. Joni is keeping an eye on them. She's so wonderful with children. And such a pleasure to be around," she added with a smile.

"Mom, don't start."

"I can't say nice things about someone without you thinking I'm trying to marry you off to her?"

"Nope, 'cause we both know you are. Here, let me finish that," Sam suggested, abandoning the argument.

"Both of you go on to the house and thaw out. I'll be up in a minute," Loretta ordered.

"You go on up, son," Tom said. "I'll stay with this stubborn woman until she's through." He dropped his left eye in a wink to Sam, then grabbed a pitchfork to help Loretta.

Sam shrugged and did as ordered. He really was cold, but he would have stayed in the barn if it would have done any good.

When he opened the kitchen door, he knew he should have stayed in the barn anyway. There was Joni, bent over from the waist to check the rolls in the oven, giving him a perfect view of her perfect derriere. Perfect.

"Ahem," he said, to alert her to his presence.

She stood and whirled in one move, a breathless

look on her face that he found even more stirring than the earlier view. "You're back!"

"Yep. Half-frozen, but we're back."

"Where's your dad? Loretta's in the barn and—"

"I know. They'll both be here in a minute. I'm going to wash up."

"I'll pour you a cup of coffee."

He stalked out of the kitchen. Did she have to fit in so perfectly? Linda hadn't wanted to lift a finger around the house, much less greet him when he came in.

The thought of Joni flying into his arms, warming his cold lips with her own, making him feel as if he was the most important man in her world, was enough to make him ignore his frozen toes. "Forget it," he warned himself, as he turned on the hot water in the downstairs bathroom and grabbed a bar of soap.

He could make it without a female cheerleader to encourage him. He was more mature than most men. He was...damn lonely.

The sad thing was, he'd been lonely married to Linda. Somehow, he'd thought his marriage would be like his parents'. They shared the ups and downs of life, laughing along the way, best friends and lovers.

He dried himself off to a stiff lecture from his conscience about remaining alone. When he reentered the kitchen, he was prepared to ignore the sexy Joni Evans.

"Coffee's on the table," she said as a greeting.

"Where are the kids?"

"We've already fed them. They're watching television. Your mother thought you might be too tired to mess with the children at lunch.''

He sighed. Too tired, yes, but they would have been a distraction. "Sleep well?''

She looked at him warily, then nodded. "Yes, thank you. And you?''

"Sure." So what was another lie? He'd tossed and turned all night, thinking about Joni, dreaming about Joni, cursing Joni.

"Were the cattle all right?''

"Fine."

Fortunately they both heard the voices of Tom and Loretta as they trudged through the snow. Since their conversation was going nowhere, maybe his parents could enliven it.

Joni poured two more cups of coffee and set them on the table. Then she took down bowls and scooped hot, savory stew into them.

"Lunch is ready," she called out as the other two came in. "I'll put the rolls on the table while you two wash up.''

"We'll be right there," Tom assured her, and the two passed through the kitchen holding hands.

"That's so sweet," she murmured, staring after them.

"What?''

"Your parents. You'd think they were newly-weds.''

He lowered his brows and trained his gaze on his cup of coffee. Especially since Joni had bent over to the oven again. This time she brought out the cookie sheet with the rolls on it and scooped them onto a plate.

When his parents came back, lunch was on the table and waiting.

"What a treat, having such service," Loretta said with a big smile.

"I didn't do much. You'd already fixed the stew, and it smells terrific. Since my taster gave it his seal of approval, I can't wait," Joni returned. "Oh, and I found the ingredients for banana pudding, so I made some. I hope that's all right."

Both older Crawfords praised her efforts.

Sam ignored her.

What else could he do? Any compliment would be interpreted as interest, for sure by his parents, maybe by Joni.

So should he refuse dessert? Naw, he wasn't that much of a masochist.

"Did you feed the kids some pudding?" Tom asked.

"Yes. Katie certainly likes it."

"Yeah, I figured. She takes after her grandpa," he agreed with a grin.

By the time they'd finished their hot stew followed by delicious banana pudding, Sam would have succumbed to a nap, preferably with Joni, if he'd had the choice. Instead he was going to drive her and Brady to their house.

"The snowplow came by about ten this morning," Loretta reported as she and Joni stacked the bowls. "And Henry did our driveway earlier."

"Then we'll be on our way as soon as you're ready, Joni," Sam said. "Shall I tell the kids?"

"Yes, please. As soon as we finish the dishes, I'll be ready."

She didn't bother to look at him, which meant he could look his fill. Until his father caught him.

"Never you mind about the dishes," Loretta said. "I'll have all afternoon to tidy up this little mess. Especially if Peter rides with y'all. Katie should be ready for her nap."

Sam shrugged. Lucky Katie.

WITH THE ROAD PLOWED, driving wasn't too bad, even if the truck did slip a little.

"I haven't done much driving on roads like this," she said finally, after a long silence between her and the driver. "In Chicago, I usually took the El."

"You'd better be sure you have snow tires on your car," he said, staring straight ahead.

Another pause.

"It was kind of your parents to make me feel so welcome."

"Folks are neighborly in Wyoming."

Dead silence, except for the boys' whisperings in the back seat.

Okay, fine. She could take a hint. Folding her arms across her chest, she stared straight ahead until he pulled to a stop in front of her house.

"Can Peter come in and see my room, Mom?" Brady asked.

"I don't know if Sam can spare the time," she

replied, putting the decision on the silent man beside her. She wasn't about to let him think she wanted him in her house.

"Sure, I can spare five minutes, Brady. But not much longer. I need to get back and help my dad."

The boys tumbled out of the truck to plow through the snow to the front porch.

"You need to hire someone to clear your sidewalk," he said as he opened his door.

She glared at him. "I'll manage."

"Do you even have a snow shovel?" he asked as he came around the front of the truck.

"Of course I do. I told you it snows a lot in Chicago." She just wasn't sure where she'd stored the shovel. Surely it was in the garage somewhere.

"Bring me the shovel and I'll get you started while I wait on Peter."

Orders, orders and more orders.

"That's all right." As if she wanted to be indebted to him. Or wanted to see his broad shoulders, strong arms, flexing in front of her. Wanted—

"Come on, Joni, you're wasting time."

She stiffened. "But it's my time, isn't it? So I can waste it if I want to."

He shot her a disgusted look. What for? Not bowing down and following his every command? Then he strode through the snow to the garage, pulled up the door and disappeared inside, leaving her standing in the snow, dumbfounded.

"What are you doing?" she demanded, hurrying after him.

He reappeared, snow shovel in hand, before she could reach him. Then, without any comment to her, he crossed to her sidewalk and began shoveling.

She debated her options. She could try to arm-wrestle the shovel away from him, but she had as much chance of success of that plan as she did of the snow melting away before bedtime.

Her second option seemed the better one. She'd go inside and hurry the boys along. And she wouldn't thank him for his efforts, either. After all, she hadn't asked for his assistance.

The boys were exploring all Brady's toys, the posters she'd put up on his wall, and the books that filled an entire shelf.

"Peter, I'm sorry, but your uncle is waiting. Why don't I call your mother and see if you can come over to play next Saturday? Then you can look at everything."

"Okay! You'll call her?" Peter asked eagerly.

"I'll call her. This afternoon, in fact. Now, put your coat back on. Your uncle's waiting."

She reminded Brady to put his coat on to accompany Peter to the truck. She didn't want any colds in their house. The three of them came to the door.

Sam, his muscles indeed flexing beneath his sheepskin coat, had almost half the sidewalk cleared.

"Peter's ready," Joni announced with determination.

Sam looked up. "Good. You two boys have a snowball fight while I finish this walk, okay?"

The boys had no difficulty following his orders, but Joni protested. "No! I mean—it's too cold."

He gave her a cool stare. Or maybe even an icy one, considering the weather. "It'll only take a couple of minutes." Then he went back to work.

Frustrated, Joni turned back into the house. She was not going to stand there and admire him. She wouldn't give him that much satisfaction!

"Mom, Sam's through!" Brady called.

If she didn't reappear, her son would think she was angry with him, not Sam.

She walked to the door. The three males were standing on the now scraped sidewalk, admiring Sam's work. She opened the door and moved to the porch. But no farther.

"Thanks, Sam."

"No problem. If you ask around, you'll find several people with snowblowers willing to clear your driveway for a couple of extra bucks."

"Thanks for the suggestion," she returned. Her words may have been gracious, but her tone wasn't. And she knew it.

His chin rose. "I'm getting a lot of thanks."

"Yes."

He took several steps closer to her, and the boys wandered toward the truck, not interested in adult matters.

"But somehow they don't sound sincere," he said softly, watching her.

"I didn't ask you to clear my walk," she said pointedly, her shoulders stiffening.

"Maybe not, but I did the job. I think I deserve a real thank-you." He came up the steps.

"I gave you a real thank-you."

"Not the kind I want."

Before she realized his intent, he pulled her against his hard chest, wrapped his arms around her and took her mouth with his.

Suddenly, instead of winter, it felt like the Fourth of July, with fireworks going off all over. His hands slid inside her jacket, under her sweater, flesh to her flesh. Hot. Wanting.

And she wanted back. Mindless, impulsive, out-of-her-head wanting.

He lifted his lips, but before she could regain her breath to protest, if that had been her intent, he settled them on hers again, at a different angle, to tease her, to lure her to greater depths.

Who knows what would have happened next, if another truck hadn't come along the almost deserted road.

"Hey, Sam!" a male voice roared. "Way to go, buddy!"

Chapter Five

"Mom, hurry! We don't want to be late," Brady called from the door to the garage.

Joni slid her feet into black pumps, grabbed her black wool coat and joined Brady. "I'm glad you want to go to Sunday School, Brady, but we have plenty of time."

"Peter will be waiting for me."

Joni rolled her eyes as her son pulled her toward their car. He climbed in and fastened his seat belt while she lifted the garage door. The driveway cleared of snow reminded her of yesterday's disaster.

Like she'd forgotten Sam's kiss.

With a weary sigh, she got into the car. If she didn't remove Sam from her life, she was never again going to get a decent night's sleep.

But she had made arrangements to have her driveway blown free of snow all winter. So Sam had actually helped her in spite of his causing her lack of sleep. She'd considered sleeping in this morning, but Brady had been eager to go to church.

Last week, their first Sunday in Saddle, they'd only

gone to the church service, not the Bible Study held beforehand. Since becoming friends with Peter, Brady was determined to attend both.

After finding the proper room for Brady and watching him reunite with Peter, Joni looked at the elderly lady who had guided them upon their arrival.

"Let's see now, dear, you'll go to the singles group. Come this way."

"You have a singles group?" Saddle was small. She'd thought the adults would be all together.

"Yes, right here."

Joni looked in the door and wanted to turn around and run. Because, of course, the singles group included Sam Crawford.

"Thank you," she murmured and slipped through the door. At the moment, Sam had his back to her, talking to some other men. If she could make it to the back row, perhaps she could avoid him altogether.

An older man, probably the teacher, saw her, however, and crossed the room to introduce himself. "Hello, I'm Jerry Williams. You must be Sam's friend."

Joni froze. The rest of the room all turned to stare at her. Sam included. Finally she said, "His family has been very friendly. Everyone in Saddle has been wonderful."

"Good, glad to hear it. Come right in. There's a seat here by Sam."

Without waiting for her to accept the invitation, he led her to a seat on the front row and called everyone to order. Sam sat down beside her.

When the class finally dismissed, Sam and Joni had not said a word to each other. But she'd been aware of his presence the entire time.

"I have to go find Brady," she said to no one in particular and almost ran from the room.

Brady was waiting impatiently. Beside him was Peter and an attractive young woman with dark hair like Peter's.

"Are you Joni?" she asked, stepping forward.

"Yes. You must be Marty."

"Yes, I'm so glad to meet you. Peter talks about Brady nonstop."

"Brady talks about Peter, too."

"Are you staying for the service?"

Joni knew what was coming. She just didn't know what to do about it.

"'Course we are," Brady said with a broad smile.

"Then why don't you join us? The boys will enjoy being together." Marty smiled warmly, and Joni couldn't say no.

She nodded and followed Sam's sister into the auditorium. After Marty introduced her husband, she let him sit by the boys. She followed him into the pew and motioned for Joni to sit beside her. When Loretta and Tom joined them, Joni breathed a sigh of relief.

Until Sam appeared at the end of the row. He tried to sit beside his father, but Loretta insisted Tom scoot to the end of the row. Then she shifted, leaving the only vacant spot beside Joni.

That's when she knew Sam was right. His mother was matchmaking.

"HAVE YOU GOTTEN your Christmas tree yet?" Marty asked after the service.

Glad to have a normal, impersonal topic, Joni smiled. "No, not yet. I'm still unpacking boxes. But we'll get one soon."

"Come with us, then. We're going to cut one down on the ranch. We do it every year and we can just as easily cut two as one."

Joni's eyes widened in horror. She had fallen into another trap. Particularly since Brady had heard the invitation.

"Yeah!" He immediately ran to Peter and informed him of the treat in store for the two of them.

"Brady!" she protested, but she knew it was already too late.

Before she could talk to her son, Loretta agreed with Marty. "Tom and I will follow you to your house so you can change."

"No. No, I need to drive so you won't have to bring me back home." She was sure of that.

"Oh, no, Joni. Tree hunting takes a long time. We don't want you driving back after dark by yourself." Without waiting for Joni to agree, she went off to find Tom.

Joni gave it one last effort. "Marty, Sam is going to be furious."

"Why?"

"Because he thinks your mother is matchmaking. I think so, too."

"It gives Mom something to do. Besides, if you don't cut down your tree, you'll have to drive to the next town to buy one. Saddle never has any trees for sale because they're all over the place.''

Tom and Loretta appeared beside her, ready to head for her house. She called to Brady, giving up the fight. At least Sam wasn't around anywhere. Maybe he didn't participate in the tree hunt.

Of course, he did.

When she and Brady arrived at the ranch, along with Tom and Loretta, Sam was waiting in the kitchen, having already been informed by Peter, she was sure.

The greeting she received could have been described as surly, if one wanted to be generous. She didn't. Crossing the room to stand beside him, she whispered fiercely, "I couldn't get out of it. This isn't my fault."

He stared at her in disbelief, only making her temper grow hotter.

"Hey, no whispering, you two," Paul called from across the room. "I certainly wasn't allowed to when I was dating Marty."

"We're not dating!" Joni and Sam said in unison.

"Well, maybe you should," Loretta said as she tied an apron around her waist.

Sam and Joni shot off in opposite directions, trying to put as much distance between them as they could. At least, Joni assumed that was Sam's intention. It certainly was hers.

During Sunday dinner, she sat between Tom and Brady and pretended Sam didn't exist. With all the conversation, it wasn't too difficult.

When she tried to help with the dishes, Loretta shooed her out of the kitchen. "Katie and I are going to stay here while the rest of you hunt for all the trees."

"All? How many are we cutting down?" Joni asked.

"One for us, one for the bunkhouse, and for you and Marty. Four in all. You'll take Tom's truck and Sam's."

Joni felt panic build in her. She turned to hurry out the door, grabbing her coat and gloves on the way. She wanted to make sure she got a seat in Tom's truck.

Too late. It was already bouncing its way across the pasture. Sam was standing beside his truck, his arms folded.

"Where are the boys?" Surely Brady and Peter would be riding with them.

"They didn't want to wait." He gave her a killer look that told her everything was her fault.

"They're all in Tom's truck?"

"Yep. Dad seemed to think it was a good idea." His words dripped with sarcasm.

"Sam, I told you, I didn't plan on coming. Marty asked me about a tree and—never mind. But it wasn't my idea."

"Doesn't matter. They're determined."

"But what can we do? Did you tell them you weren't interested?"

He uncrossed his arms and put his hands on his

hips. "Lady, I have told everyone in Saddle. But it doesn't seem to make any difference."

"Well, don't blame me. I'm not the one who grabbed someone and kissed them in front of the entire town!" She was not going to be blamed for his difficulties.

He didn't pretend to be innocent. "I know. That was a big mistake."

"It certainly was!"

"'Cause I want to do the same thing again."

She couldn't believe he'd said that. And she took a step back just to be cautious.

"Don't worry. I know better. Mom's watching out the kitchen window. So get in the truck and let's go find those stupid trees." He strode around the truck, got in and slammed the door. Waiting for her.

Joni finally opened the passenger door, got in and closed it. Then she clung to it as if it were a lifeline.

"What are we going to do?" she finally asked as they followed in Tom's path.

"I'll take care of it. I've got a plan."

She shot him a curious stare. "Do you want to tell me about it?"

"Nope."

She glared at him. "Then how can I help?"

"I'm not sure your help would be all that beneficial. After all, you're here, aren't you?" He stared straight ahead.

Heat surged through her. If he wasn't driving, she'd slap his face. She'd already told him it wasn't her fault. Clearly he didn't believe her.

SAM WATCHED JONI as she picked the first tree they came to. He'd made her mad and she wasn't going to prolong her visit.

Good. He had enough to deal with without the temptation of kissing her.

"No, Mom," Brady protested. "It's too little."

"And has a big hole in the back," Marty added. "Let's look at that one on the hill." She led the charge up the snow-covered hill.

Paul looked at Joni. "I should've warned you. They seek perfection. At least we're not out in a driving snowstorm like last year."

"A snowstorm? And they still were picky?" she asked in disbelief.

Though his eyes were twinkling, Paul nodded solemnly. "Great family. But they're nuts about their Christmas trees." Then he followed his wife up the hill.

Janie looked around in exasperation until she seemed to realize she and Sam were the only ones left standing near the trucks. Without a word, she ran after the others.

"Like I was a grizzly bear, threatening her," Sam muttered to himself. Okay, so he hadn't been exactly nice in the truck. But after that kiss yesterday, he was on guard. The lady packed a real punch, and half the town considered them a couple already.

He'd thought about finding her a man before. But it had been a halfhearted idea. Now he had no choice. He really was going to matchmake. Because if he didn't find Brady a daddy for Christmas, he was going to be in big trouble.

When he reached the top of the hill, he discovered an argument in progress.

"No, Brady. It is definitely too big."

"Mom, it won't touch the ceiling." Suddenly spying Sam, he asked him to verify his words.

"Probably not. Looks to be about seven feet. Right, Dad?"

"Right, son. Don't you like it, Joni?"

"It's beautiful, Tom, but I'd have a hard time getting it in the Christmas tree stand. Something smaller would be better."

"I'll put it in the stand for you." Sam couldn't blame Joni for the incredulous look she shot him after their conversation in the truck. But it was a Christmas tree. And it was Brady's choice.

"Good enough," Tom said. "Who's going to chop it down?"

"I will," Sam said. "Go look for three more so we can get home before our toes freeze."

The others, minus Joni and Brady, tromped farther up the hill.

"What are you doing?" Joni demanded in a low voice.

"Chopping down your tree, hurrying up the process. I'm cold." But he was getting warmer the closer she came.

"Can I help?" Brady demanded, interrupting their whispering.

"Maybe in a couple of years, son," Sam said with

a smile. "Axes are kind of dangerous. Move over there with your mom while I cut the tree down."

His ax was sharp and it only took five or six swings to fell the tree. "Okay, Brady, now you can help. We'll drag the tree to my truck."

The boy was delighted to be included, and Sam sensed some of the anger leaving Joni. He gave her a sideways grin. She was such a good mother, he knew she could always be charmed by kindnesses to her son.

But that wasn't why he let Brady help. It was Brady's Christmas tree. He should get to help. His father should be letting him help. But until he got a father, Sam would share Christmas with him.

THREE MORE TREES were quickly found, a record Paul assured everyone. As soon as they reached the ranch house, Joni insisted Sam take her and Brady, and their tree, home. She resisted Loretta's persistent arguments that they stay and decorate the family tree.

Sam wasn't going to be able to accuse her of trying to stay close to him.

She even silenced Brady with a sharp command when he began to whine. With a sigh, she ruffled his head, offering a silent apology. But when he appeared ready to argue again, she gave him her sternest look.

At the house, she dragged out the tree stand, packed away in the garage, and took it outside to Sam.

"You go on inside," Sam ordered. "Brady and I will have the tree ready in a few minutes."

More orders. That's all the man did, give her orders.

"I'm perfectly able to help."

"I have Brady to help. I don't need anyone else," Sam said evenly, staring at her.

She looked down at her son and read the pride in his eyes. "Okay, since you have such good help," she said, smiling at her son.

Once inside, she put on a pot of hot chocolate. It was the least she could do. But she'd offer to make Sam's to go. He deserved that, even if he was being sweet to Brady.

When they brought the tree inside, Joni showed him where to put it.

"Will you help us decorate it?" Brady asked, hopping up and down in excitement.

Both adults answered together. "No."

Joni quickly added, "I made hot chocolate. If you don't have time to stay and drink it, I have a foam cup."

The difficult man refused to escape. "I have time to drink some."

She left him standing in the living room. "Fine."

"Hey, Mom!" Brady called after her. "Bring marshmallows, too. Sam loves marshmallows."

She plunked down a bowl and filled it with marshmallows. She hoped they all went to fat at once on the lean cowboy. It would serve him right.

When she carried the tray into the living room, Brady and Sam were staring at the tree.

"What's wrong?"

"Nothing," Sam drawled. "We were just trying to decide if this is the tree's best side. What do you think?"

"I think it looks perfect. Here's the chocolate."

"And marshmallows, Sam," Brady added, pushing the bowl closer to his guest.

"Thanks, son," Sam replied with a smile.

"Stop calling him that!" she ordered, unable to hold back her irritation.

Sam stared at her, as if she'd lost her mind.

"I like it, Mom," Brady protested.

She wished she'd never spoken. "Is your chocolate too hot, Brady? I brought some extra milk to cool it down."

"Yes, please," he said, but she could tell he hadn't forgiven her comment.

"Thank you for your help today, Sam. We're pretty well set now. I shouldn't have to bother you for anything in the future." That should tell him she wasn't going to cling.

"It was no bother. Brady's a good helper, so it went fast."

Brady puffed out his narrow chest and flexed one arm. "I'm really strong, aren't I?" He looked at Sam. "This is how you show your muscle. Show me yours, Sam."

Joni tried not to look as Sam, having shed his coat, flexed his muscle for Brady. The seam on his shirt-sleeve strained as he did so.

"Mom doesn't have much muscle. Show him, Mom," Brady ordered, scorn in his voice.

"No, sweetie, I don't think so."

"You afraid to be called a weakling?" Sam asked, a smile on his firm lips.

Unfair. She didn't like to resist a challenge. Without too much thought, she flexed her muscle.

"I reckon I'll have to feel it since you're wearing that thick sweater," Sam said.

Before she could pull her arm away, he settled his warm hand around it and gently squeezed.

"Hey, Brady, she does have some muscle. Kind of puny, but at least it's there."

Brady giggled. "Mine's bigger."

The phone rang and Brady set down his chocolate and dashed into the kitchen, calling, "I'll get it," over his shoulder.

Joni's eyes widened in alarm. She jerked her arm from Sam's hold. "I—I think you should leave before—"

"Mom, it's Peter. I'm going to talk, okay?" Brady called from the kitchen.

"Yes, okay," she called back. Then she started again. "I think you should leave before Brady comes back."

"Yeah, you're right," Sam said, taking one more sip of his chocolate and then standing.

"Thank you for your help, but we won't be needing anything else. We won't bother you." Her voice was breathless as she also stood. Too close to Sam. She took a step back.

To her surprise, he took hold of both her arms and tugged her forward.

"Sam! What are you—"

Doing? What was he doing? He was kissing her, as he had yesterday on her porch. All thoughts disappeared as sensations took over.

Then he released her and stepped back.

"I thought I deserved one more kiss before I put my plan into action." Then he turned around and walked out, leaving a stunned Joni staring after him.

What plan?

It couldn't be any more devastating than his kiss.

Chapter Six

Wednesday, Sam was ready to put his plan into action.

He figured by midnight tonight, his problems would be over. Joni would have a man in her life. Brady would have a potential father.

Sam would be left alone.

He stepped into the classroom after a lot of children ran past him. Expecting to find Joni alone, as he had before, he was surprised to discover another woman sitting beside her desk.

"Oh, uh, excuse me," he muttered as both women looked up.

"Why, Sam Crawford," the woman said, and he recognized Elsie Perkins, an old school chum. "I heard you were sniffing around Mrs. Evans, but I didn't know anything would get you off the ranch during the week."

Damn! It was a good thing he had a plan.

Joni tried to help out. "I'm sure he's here about his nephew, Mrs. Perkins. Peter and my son are great friends."

"Yeah, right," the woman replied, laughing. "Well, thanks for your help, Mrs. Evans. I'll try your suggestion tonight. So long, Sam."

Sam stayed by the door until he could see Elsie leave the building. Then he faced Joni's glare.

"Sorry. I thought you'd be alone."

"What do you want?"

She didn't sound welcoming. He understood why, but contrarily, it irritated him. "I'm trying to fix things, but you don't seem too appreciative."

"I wonder why."

Time to cut to the chase. Before her big brown eyes lured him closer. "I'm going to take you and Brady out for pizza tonight."

"Thanks for the gracious invitation," she said, arching her brows, "but no thanks."

"This is part of my plan," he emphasized, stepping closer.

"Being seen together will make people stop talking about us? I don't think much of your logic. If we just ignore each other, the talk will die down, Sam. That's the best way." She started organizing papers on her desk.

Like she could just ignore him.

"No, it's not. My way is best." He was sure of that. After all, Brady wanted a father, deserved a father. He was a great kid.

And Sam had to have a good reason not to sleep with Joni.

She gave him a sugary smile. "I wouldn't know,

since you haven't bothered to share your plan with me.'' Then she went back to shuffling her papers.

"Can't you just trust me?" he asked, moving closer to her desk.

"You didn't trust me when I told you my being there Sunday wasn't my fault."

He leaned over and put his hands on top of her papers, stopping her movement and forcing her to look at him. "Yes, I did. I apologize. I was frustrated and took my anger out on you. That was wrong."

He didn't like to apologize, but if he was going to, he wanted to do it right. Her brown eyes softened, and her full lips gentled.

"That was a nice apology. Thank you."

"It's the truth," he added with a smile. "So, will you trust me tonight? Will you and Brady come with me for pizza?"

"Why?"

"I think things will go better if you don't ask. You'll get a free meal."

He lost some of the ground he'd gained as she glared at him. "Brady and I are not charity cases! I can pay for our meals. In fact, I'll go, but only if we go dutch."

He leaned a little closer, his gaze on those soft lips. "Sweetheart, the cost of the pizza isn't a big deal. But we've got to get our lives straightened out before someone gets hurt."

He was thinking of Brady, of course, but Joni's cheeks flushed with color.

She looked away. "Okay. What time shall we

come to the pizza parlor?'' There was only one in
Saddle.

''I'll pick you up at six-thirty. And wear something
pretty.'' Unable to resist, he leaned over and gave her
a quick kiss. Then he hightailed it out of there before
he gave in to temptation and hauled her out of the
chair into his arms.

JONI WAS SURE she'd made a mistake.

If she'd read Sam's request about her attire cor-
rectly, she was to dress as if they were on a date. And
she didn't see how the evening would solve their
problem.

Even so, she chose a soft blue wool dress with long
sleeves and a scooped neck, one of her favorites. She
curled her hair and pulled it back on the sides with
combs.

When she felt she was looking her best, she went
searching for Brady. She hadn't yet told him of the
treat in store for him.

''Wow, Mom, you look pretty,'' he exclaimed
when she came to the door of his room.

''Thank you, son. Um, are you hungry?''

''Sure. Is dinner ready?''

''We're going out for dinner. Go wash your hands
and comb your hair.''

''Are we going to the ranch?'' he asked, excitement
building in his voice.

''No.''

''Oh. I haven't seen Sam since we put up the tree.

And he hasn't seen it since we decorated it. He'll really like it, Mom. Maybe if you called him he'd—''

She couldn't take any more, so she interrupted him. "Sam will be here in ten minutes."

"Wow!" Brady exclaimed and leaped to his feet. "I'll go turn on the Christmas lights!"

"Brady, I'll turn on the lights. You go wash up."

With a sigh, she went to the living room and plugged in the lights she'd strung on the tree Monday night.

Almost before she'd finished, Brady came barreling down the hall. "Mom, you know what Peter said today?"

Since most of Brady's conversation was full of reference to Peter, she wasn't surprised. "No. What did Peter say?"

"If you and Sam got married, we'd be brothers!"

Joni froze, alarm spreading through her. "Brady— Brady, Sam and I aren't going to get married. And you and Peter wouldn't be brothers even if we did."

"But Peter said—"

"If Sam and I married, the two of you would be cousins. But that's not going to happen. So you get to be best friends. Isn't that just as good?"

"Why can't you marry Sam?"

Her child was nothing if not stubborn. "People marry because they love each other. And Sam and I don't love each other." She didn't even want to think of the man in terms of love.

"Can't you try?" Brady pleaded.

She bent down and kissed her son's cheek. Sadly

she said, "No, baby, you can't try to love someone. It just happens." But you could try not to love someone. That was a definite possibility.

A knock on the door stopped the conversation.

Before she went to open the door, however, she cautioned her son. "Don't say anything to Sam about what we just talked about. Okay?"

Brady nodded.

She swung open the door, the sight of the handsome cowboy making her catch her breath.

He nodded to her and stepped into their living room. His attention moved to Brady after his gaze covered her from top to toe. "Nice looking Christmas tree, Brady. I could see the lights from the street."

Brady beamed. "Thanks. I wanted Mom to put lights up outside, but she said she couldn't."

"You should've called me," Sam said, turning to Joni. "I would—"

"I'm sure you were busy," she said firmly. "Besides, I think our tree will provide us with plenty of Christmas spirit."

"Yes, of course," Sam said, nodding in agreement. "Well, are you ready for pizza, Brady?"

"Sure. I love pizza. Is Peter coming?"

"No, I'm afraid it'll just be the three of us. Unless we run into someone we know."

Joni noticed that Sam didn't look at either of them as he added that last sentence. What was going on?

He led the way out to his truck, after they unplugged the Christmas lights, much to Brady's disappointment. "It wouldn't be safe, son," Sam said, his hand on Brady's shoulder.

Joni sighed. She'd already voiced her displeasure that he called her child son. She figured his careless term of affection only added to Brady's dreams.

When they reached the pizza parlor, Sam, after asking Joni about her preferences, told her he and Brady would go place their order. She could choose a table.

More orders. The man assumed she would go along with whatever he said. And she did, she had to admit. Granted, he had to reason with her for their outing tonight. But he'd won.

She chose a table against the wall, out of the traffic pattern of people arriving and ordering. In spite of Sam's assurance that he had a plan, she wasn't anxious to be spotted by the gossips of Saddle.

He and Brady found her. He set their drinks on the table, then looked around. "It's kind of dark at this table. Don't you want to sit closer to the center of the—I mean, where there's more light?"

Yes, there was definitely something going on.

"I like it here," she said calmly, not moving.

"Okay," he agreed, drawing out the word as he settled into a chair across from her, with Brady between them.

"Sam ordered two big pizzas," Brady said, seemingly impressed with that much pizza.

"Two large pizzas? You must be starving," she said to Sam.

"Uh, yeah, well, I wanted to have plenty of pizza

in case Brady here needs more. He's a growing boy, you know."

With those heavy hints, Joni wasn't surprised when Sam hailed another man as if he were a savior just after their pizza was delivered to their table.

"Billy! I haven't seen you in weeks. What are you doing here?"

Since the man was standing in the center of the room, looking as if he was searching for someone and stopped looking as soon as Sam hailed him, her suspicions were confirmed.

"Joni, let me introduce you to Billy Hawkins. He has a spread about thirty miles outside town. Join us, Billy. I ordered too much pizza and we need help eating it."

"Don't mind if I do," the man replied with a big grin and plopped down in the empty chair.

The next half hour was trying for Joni. Though she wasn't sure why. The man was muscular, almost as tall as Sam, friendly, intelligent. She had nothing against him. Except she was being pitched to him as if she was the snake oil those traveling salesmen used to sell as cure-alls.

As soon as Brady finished his pizza, Sam invited him to play a video game with him on the other side of the restaurant. Brady, of course, didn't hesitate.

Once they were alone, silence fell between Joni and Billy. Finally the man leaned forward. "I, uh, wondered if you'd like to go into Lander to see a movie this Friday. They've got a real nice theater and it's only about a forty-five-minute drive...unless it snows, of course.''

Joni was prepared. ''That's very kind of you, Billy, but since we just moved here and Christmas is around the corner, I really don't have any extra time for socializing. Besides, I'm not interested in dating.''

''But Sam said—'' he began, then stopped.

''I know. But Sam didn't understand the situation. His parents are matchmaking and he's afraid I'll cooperate.'' Her voice hardened. ''But he has nothing to worry about.''

Billy stared at his plate of half-eaten pizza before he raised his gaze to her face again. ''You know, I came tonight because of Sam. But I asked you out because I want to get to know you better.'' He stood to leave. ''After you get settled in, let me know if you change your mind.''

SAM ONLY KEPT HALF of his attention on the video game. The other half was on Joni and Billy across the restaurant. He frowned when Billy reached across the table to touch Joni. His friend was moving a little fast.

He'd have a talk with him.

Then he realized Billy was saying goodbye.

''Sam?'' Brady said.

''Uh, yeah, son?''

''Why is that man staying with Mom?''

''He wanted to get to know her,'' he said, staring at Joni as she now sat alone. Maybe he should've explained his plan, but he was afraid she'd feel awkward. Instead he had a sinking feeling she hadn't cooperated.

"Your mom's alone now. We need to go back to the table."

Brady asked to finish his game, and Sam couldn't think of a reason not to.

Until a man sat down at the table next to Joni and struck up a conversation. Damn, it wasn't safe to leave her alone.

He hurried Brady back to the table.

"I'm still hungry," he announced loudly, staring at the stranger.

"There's plenty of pizza left." Joni didn't crack a smile.

The stranger nodded to Sam. "Sorry to interrupt. Your wife was giving me directions."

"She's not—" Brady began, but Sam covered his mouth with a big hand.

"He was going to say his mom's not good with directions, but that wasn't tactful, Brady." He smiled at Joni, but she didn't respond. "She has other talents."

Those words got a response. Her cheeks reddened and her gaze sparkled with anger. But maybe the stranger would think it was affection. Yeah, maybe.

"Ready to go, honey?" he asked, figuring he'd better get her out of there before she exploded.

"I thought you wanted to eat more pizza?" she asked, staring at him.

"Brady, go get one of those boxes. We'll take it home with us." As the boy ran to do his bidding, he took one of Joni's hands and pulled her to her feet. "Come on, sweetheart, it's time to go home."

She wasn't happy with him. "Your home or mine?" she muttered, but he didn't think the man heard her. Brady returned with the box and he slid in the slices of pizza. "Well, let's go," he said, slipping his free hand around Joni's shoulder.

Startled, she stared at him, but he ignored her response. Until they started toward the door and ran into one of his mother's friends, Mrs. Elkins.

"Why, Sam, I haven't seen you in ages. And who is your ladyfriend? I hadn't heard you were on the prowl again."

Joni looked at him as if she thought he deserved exactly what he'd gotten. Maybe she was right.

"IT'S YOUR FAULT for turning down Billy. I was going to excuse myself and let him take you home."

She couldn't believe the gall of the man. "My fault? I didn't even know what was going on, because you hadn't told me. If you had, I could've explained that I wouldn't accept a date from Billy."

"What's wrong with Billy?" Sam demanded in a loud roar.

Joni closed her eyes briefly. Then she stared at Sam. "There's nothing wrong with Billy. But you'll be explaining that to Brady if you don't lower your voice."

Sam had brought them home, come in and visited with Brady until his bedtime. Now that Brady was safely tucked away, Joni was trying to work out their difficulties.

Without much success.

He did as she asked, responding with a low growl. "But you've messed things up. If we don't hook you up with someone else, we're going to end up together."

She tried to ignore the pain his words dealt her. After all, she wasn't looking for a husband. But being rejected wasn't pleasant. "Your mistake, Sam, was assuming I would cooperate with your parents. That I wanted a husband."

"Don't you?"

"No."

"Why not? Brady is a great kid and deserves a father."

"Of course he deserves a father, a good, loving father, but I can't marry the first man off the street for Brady's sake. That wouldn't work."

"Why? Billy's a good guy."

Frustrated, she abandoned her calm reasoning. "Fine! You marry him!"

He grabbed her arms and pulled her closer. "You're being ridiculous!"

"Yes, I am, because I can't get you to understand. You can't go around ordering other people's lives. I'm not going to marry, and I don't want to date anyone. I'll leave you alone, and everyone will catch on eventually that we're not a couple."

"How long will it take Brady to catch on?"

That was hitting below the belt. She bent her head

and it rested on Sam's chest. "I don't know. I told him not to say anything to you."

"He didn't. But Peter thought his idea was worth sharing."

Wearily she lifted her head. "I'll talk to him again."

"But he wants a daddy, sweetheart. If you'd try dating, just a little, he'd realize I'm not the only prospect. And you might find someone you like."

She already had. That idea flashed through her mind before she could shut it down. It was the truth. She liked Sam. With any encouragement, she'd love Sam. But Sam was going to great effort to tell her he wasn't interested.

Maybe she should do as he asked.

"Fine. I'll look for someone to—to date."

"I'll take care of it," he assured her.

"I can find my own dates, Sam. I'm sure that man tonight would've asked me out if you hadn't shown up at the table when you did."

"Yeah," he agreed, irritation in his voice. "I'm sure he would've, too, but it wouldn't be safe."

"Fine. I'll be careful, take my time and choose someone nice."

"We don't have much time. Christmas is two and a half weeks away," he insisted, squeezing her shoulders.

"Sam, I don't have to be dating someone by Christmas. Brady isn't going to get a daddy for Christmas. He'll have to understand that."

"But you could at least start seeing someone. Friday night—no, I know. Saturday night, we'll double-date. Mom will keep Brady for you. When he sees me with another woman and you with another man, he'll understand.''

He had a point. Until Brady saw Sam with another woman, he'd probably think his mother was just being uncooperative. ''Fine. If you can set that up, I'll go along. But not Billy. He's too nice to play games with.''

''Right. I'll take care of it. Saturday night we'll have everything taken care of. Do you have a preference as to what kind of man—I mean, mostly we have cowboys and ranchers. There's a mechanic or two and—I know. The vet. He'll be perfect.''

''A veterinarian? He's not married?''

''Nope. You'll like him. His name is Donald.''

She hated the name Donald. But she wasn't going to say so. After all, what she liked wasn't the point.

''Okay. That will be fine.''

She must not have shown enough enthusiasm in her response. He squeezed her shoulders again, pulling her just that much closer. ''It'll be all right, Joni. He's a nice man.''

''I'm sure he is.''

''He's a friend,'' he added, but Joni didn't understand his point.

Sam spoke again. ''I would never betray a friend.''

She stared up at him, puzzled.

''That's why I'm going to kiss you now. Because, after Saturday, when you're Donald's girl, I can't ever kiss you again.''

Chapter Seven

"Merry Christmas, Mrs. Evans," the children shouted as the bell rang on Friday. Christmas vacation was only one week away, and they were all excited about the coming holiday.

"Not yet, class. I'll see you on Monday," she returned as they left the classroom.

When all the children had disappeared, she slumped back in her chair. She'd been on the job two weeks, and she felt quite settled in. However, she, too, was looking forward to Christmas vacation. Since she'd started work as soon as they arrived in Saddle, she'd had little time to spare. Another week, and she could organize her house, do a little shopping.

Prepare for a new year.

Without Sam.

How could the man have become so important to her in such a short time? Maybe it had something to do with those incredible kisses. When he'd grabbed her Wednesday night, she'd told herself to resist. Until their lips met, his warm hands caressed her, his body pressed against hers.

"Joni?"

She started and turned toward the door.

Mary Bledsoe, the other second-grade teacher, was staring at her. "Are you all right? Your face is flushed."

"I'm fine." She hurriedly changed the subject. "Are you ready for Christmas?"

Mary was a quiet, shy woman about Joni's age. Unmarried. Joni hoped they would become friends as the year progressed.

"I thought I was, but…last night, Sam Crawford called me."

Uh-oh. Joni braced herself. "Really? Are the two of you friends?"

"Not exactly. I mean, we know each other, of course, since we both grew up here, but…anyway, he asked me to help him out by going into Lander to dinner and the movies Saturday night." She stared at Joni, a question in her look. "He said you and Donald Steel would be going with us."

"Um, yes," Joni said, rearranging things on her desk. "Sam mentioned an outing like that. It'll be fun, won't it?"

"I guess. But since I don't go out much, I thought I should see what you're wearing."

Joni hadn't given her wardrobe any thought. She'd been doing too much thinking about Sam's kisses. "I'll probably wear a sweater and a skirt, not too dressy, not too casual. Does that sound all right to you?"

"Oh, you'd know better than me. I don't have much of a social life." Mary sounded apologetic.

"I think most people just pretend to have a big social life, Mary. I haven't dated since my husband died."

"Except for Sam."

Joni choked. "Uh, I'm not dating Sam. He's just been helpful since we moved here."

"Oh."

Joni was feeling more and more confused. Why had Mary accepted a date with Sam if she thought he was interested in someone else? But she didn't know Mary well enough to ask that question.

"Did Sam mention what movie we're going to see?" Joni couldn't think of anything else to ask.

"No."

"Well, I'm sure it will be fun." She smiled, then thought of something else. "Do you know Donald?"

"Not really. I've seen him. But I'm sure I'll like him. It will be so nice to have something to do. I have to go, but I'll see you tomorrow night."

Joni stared at the place Mary had been. She was sure she'd like Donald? What had Sam done?

SAM HAD EVERYTHING arranged.

He'd picked up Donald Steel first. He thought he should tell the other man about some of Joni's likes and dislikes. Donald had listened intently. That was a good sign.

Of course, when they picked up Mary, she'd insisted on getting in the back seat, saying the leg room was better for the men up front. He'd borrowed his mother's car, a Lincoln Town Car, so they'd have plenty of room. But Mary was still sitting primly in the back seat.

Probably they'd all trade places when Joni joined them.

He pulled up in front of Joni's little house and looked at Donald. When the man didn't move, he said, "You want to go see if Joni's ready?"

"Oh, yeah, sure."

He and Mary sat there in silence. He didn't know what to say to her. He'd already told her she looked nice.

Fortunately the door opened almost immediately and Brady raced down the sidewalk. "Hey, Sam!"

He waved to the boy and watched as Donald held open the back door of the car. Brady slid in, followed by Joni. Okay, so they'd start out with the ladies in the back seat. They still had to drop off Brady at his mother's.

He'd intentionally planned it that way so Brady would see him with another woman. His mother had asked Brady to spend the night, telling Joni she'd bring him to church in the morning. This was the only way Brady would know that Sam was on a date with Mary.

Except now he didn't know.

Because Donald was sitting in the front seat.

Sam frowned. But he couldn't think of anything else to do.

"Where's your truck, Sam?" Brady asked. He was holding his overnight bag on his lap.

"It's at home. I thought we'd use the car for the ladies. They'd be cramped in the back seat of the truck."

"Girls, yuck!" Brady said.

"Young man, you'd better remember who cooks your meals and washes your clothes," Joni warned, but she was smiling.

Sam kept trying to think of ways to show Brady that Mary was his date as he drove to the ranch, but nothing came to mind. Mary wasn't a flirt, so she didn't help the situation any.

Joni got out with Brady and walked to the door, knocking on it. Loretta opened it and spoke briefly, then sent Joni back to the car. Brady didn't show any hesitation at staying with Sam's mom.

"It's so nice that Brady gets along with your parents," Mary said.

"Uh, yeah," Sam agreed, but his mind was spinning. Why would Mary say that?

"Ready," Joni said as she got back into the car. "What movie are we going to see?"

Her question distracted him and he explained their choices. Both women voted for the latest romantic comedy. He'd expected as much. Besides, he hoped it would give Donald some ideas.

The restaurant he'd chosen had several cozy booths, but Donald asked for a table for four, explaining that he always felt claustrophobic in a booth. Mary surprisingly agreed with him.

During dinner, Sam noticed that Mary and Donald seemed to have a lot in common. He'd always thought Mary a shy woman, quiet, but tonight she chatted with Donald about his customers and their pets, particularly when some of them were the parents of her students.

Sam took another bite of his steak, watching the two of them. Finally he turned to Joni, sitting on his right. He noticed a smile playing around the edges of her lips. Lips that were eminently kissable.

"What's going on here?" he whispered.

"I think you didn't make things clear," she returned, her breath teasing his ear.

Frowning, he said, "Of course I did. I told them the four of us would go out."

"That's what I thought." Joni straightened in her chair and smiled at the other two, who were watching them. "Do you like the actor in the movie we're going to see, Mary?"

"Oh, yes, he's so romantic. And handsome. I like men with blond hair, don't you?"

Sam frowned again. That wasn't a good sign. Donald had blond hair, not him. Not that he wanted Mary to fall for him, but in terms of the evening... No, it wasn't a good sign.

"Actually I prefer dark-haired men," Joni said with a smile. "Not that you're not attractive, Donald."

"Everyone has their preference. I happen to like brunettes," he said, ducking his head.

Mary's cheeks reddened, but she smiled, one hand going to her brunette curls.

Donald leaned across the table. "How about you, Sam?"

Lost in his worries, Sam stared at Donald blankly. "How about me what?"

"Do you prefer blondes or brunettes?"

He stared at Joni's blond curls before turning back to Donald. "I prefer redheads," he snapped.

Joni took a sip of her tea. "Good. A hot-tempered redhead is what you deserve." She pushed back her chair. "Excuse me."

"Oh," Mary said, as if Joni had startled her. "I'll go with you."

JONI WONDERED if Sam would try to explain Donald's role to him while the women were absent from the table. But when she and Mary came back, both men were talking to a third she didn't know.

Sam and Donald stood and pulled out their chairs before Sam introduced Joni to the visitor, a rancher from the area.

"Jed came by just after you ladies excused yourselves," Sam said, giving Joni a speaking look.

"Right," the man said with a hearty laugh. "I guess I'd better make myself scarce now that you pretty ladies are back. Nice to see you, Sam. You, too, Donald." With a wave, he strolled away.

Joni hid her smile. Sam sounded frustrated. She'd considered trying to hint to Mary, but then she'd thought better of it. This plan was Sam's, not hers.

When they reached the theater, they discovered a long line at the ticket booth.

Sam pulled out his wallet. "You ladies go on in and get in line for popcorn and drinks, and we'll get the tickets." He handed Joni, who was standing closest to him, some money.

"No popcorn for me," Donald said. "I have to watch my cholesterol."

"Me, neither," Mary said when they went inside. "Just get some for you and Sam."

Joni wasn't about to pass up popcorn. That was part of going to a movie. She got one large popcorn and four drinks, and waited for the men.

"Let's go," Sam said, taking his drink. "I think the movie's crowded."

They all stepped into the semidarkness. The theater was almost full.

"I think we'll have to split up," Donald whispered.

"But—but I only got one popcorn," Joni protested.

"That's okay. Mary said she didn't want any, either," Donald said. Then he took Mary's arm and headed down the aisle.

Joni stared at them. She shouldn't have been surprised, but she was. She looked at Sam.

"Do you think they didn't understand? Or was it the popcorn?" Sam asked wryly. "I assume you like popcorn?"

"I can't stand to watch a movie without it."

"Neither can I. Come on, let's find a couple of seats."

They squeezed into two seats in the middle of a row only three back from Donald and Mary.

"There they are," Joni whispered after they were seated.

Sam put the popcorn between them and then took a handful. "I don't think it matters anymore."

"Why?" Joni asked.

"Because they're obviously interested in each other. Neither of us could get a word in edgewise at the restaurant. I bet he rides in the back seat going home."

"Maybe if you explained—"

"Nope. It's too late. I'll think of someone else, but for tonight, we might as well relax and enjoy ourselves."

Since the previews began at that moment, Joni decided Sam was right. They shared the popcorn and whispered comments about the future movies. Then, when the main feature began, Sam slid his arm around her shoulders and pulled her against him.

Oh, yes, she was enjoying herself.

WHEN THE MOVIE ENDED, Sam reluctantly moved away from Joni. The movie had been good. Holding her against him had been better. They waited in the lobby for Donald and Mary.

The couple came out with their arms wrapped around each other. Even when they saw Joni and Sam waiting, they didn't pull apart.

Nope, they definitely hadn't understood.

"Ready?" Sam asked. When Donald nodded, Sam

took Joni's hand and led the way. They shrugged into their coats and headed for the car.

Just as Sam had predicted, Donald and Mary got into the back seat. Five minutes into the ride home, Donald and Mary were getting very friendly in the back seat.

Joni turned around once to initiate some conversation, but she quickly faced front again, her cheeks red. Sam reached out and touched her.

"Come over here. I'm lonely."

She hesitated, but then she undid her seat belt and slid over next to him, fastening the center belt. "Aren't you worried about giving them the wrong impression?" she whispered.

"Sweetheart, I'm not sure they even remember we're in the car. And if I don't get us home soon, I'm afraid we're both going to be embarrassed."

They didn't talk much more, but Sam wrapped his arm around her shoulders, as he'd done in the theater. She fit against him perfectly, as if she'd always belonged there.

Without any discussion, he dropped Mary and Donald off first. Then he drove much more slowly to Joni's house.

Her head was resting on his shoulder when he stopped the car. Had she gone to sleep? "Joni, we're home."

Abruptly she straightened. "Oh, thanks. It was a lovely evening. I'm sorry things didn't—"

"I'll take you in, make sure everything's all right," he said and opened his car door.

"That's really not necessary," Joni called as he circled the car.

By the time he reached her side she had her door open and was getting out. "Really, Sam, I'll be fine. You don't need to come in."

He ignored her, catching her hand in his, as he had at the movie theater, and pulled her up the walk behind him, then waited quietly while she dug out her keys.

Once they were inside, he walked through the house, making sure no one was there. It wasn't that they had a lot of crime in Saddle. He didn't want to leave.

She remained in the living room. Pausing at the door, he stared at her. She was studying the Christmas tree, with its lights unplugged, but he found Joni more interesting.

Quietly he stepped behind her and wrapped his arms around her. He felt her jump in surprise.

"Shh," he whispered, ducking his head so they stood with their cheeks pressed together.

Joni leaned back against him, but she said, "Sam, we shouldn't do this."

"I'm only holding you. I've tried to give you away, but you keep coming back to me."

She stiffened. "I'm not a book, or a—a coin. You don't have the right to give me away because you've never had me!"

He groaned. "Don't I know it. But I'm willing to have you, sweetheart, for a night. And we'd both wake up a lot more satisfied than we are right now."

She broke free from his hold. "I'm not interested."

"Do you intend to remain celibate the rest of your life?" he asked, watching her, wanting her.

"I don't know." She moved farther away. "But I think making love should mean more than—than lust."

The problem was, he did, too. And it would, if he and Joni made love. Which meant it was a good thing she resisted. "You're right. I'll go now."

She turned and stared at him and he wasn't sure if she was happy or sad about his agreement.

"Thank you," she said softly and opened the door for him.

Okay, so he was going. But he ought to have at least a kiss. He dipped his head and brushed her lips with his. Nothing deep, but it stirred more hunger. He exited in a hurry, before that hunger could make him change his mind.

He hurried down the sidewalk and got into the car. Slipping the key into the ignition, he turned it, already reaching for his seat belt as he did.

Nothing.

He frowned, then turned it again.

Still nothing.

He checked all the dials, but he couldn't see a problem. When he turned on the radio, however, he discovered the battery must be dead. He didn't know why the battery should choose now to die.

He just knew it was really bad timing.

He got out and opened the trunk. If his mother had jumper cables, he could get Joni to give him a boost.

No jumper cables.

With a sigh, he trudged back up the sidewalk and knocked on the door.

Joni opened it after a couple of minutes. "What's wrong?"

"The battery is dead. Do you have jumper cables?"

She stared at him, her eyes wide. Then she shook her head. "No."

"Damn."

"What do we do now?" she asked.

"I could call Dad, but it's almost one o'clock." He waited, but she said nothing. "Look, if I promise to keep my distance, could I stay here until morning?"

"Sam, you'll never convince anyone, especially your parents, that we're not dating if you stay here. Everyone will see that car and—"

"Damn it! I know that. You want me to stay in the car all night? I'll be a Popsicle in the morning if I do."

"No, of course not, but—" She sighed and shrugged her shoulders. "Of course you can spend the night."

She swung the door wider for him to enter.

He did so before she could change her mind.

"I'll put clean sheets on my bed," she said and walked out of the living room.

Sam stared after her. Had she changed her mind about sleeping with him? He hurried after her.

"Joni, I didn't mean—you don't have to share your

bed. I'll sleep on the couch.'' He'd prefer to share with her, but not if that wasn't what she wanted.

"Share with you? I'm not going to share with you!" she said, astonishment in her gaze. "I'm going to sleep in Brady's bed. It's too small for you."

"Oh. Of course. I didn't realize—I can sleep on the couch. I don't want to put you out."

"I'll be comfortable in Brady's bed." She continued to strip the sheets off her bed. Then she walked past him to put them in the clothes hamper. When she returned with clean sheets, he shook himself from his stupor and took one corner of the bottom sheet to help her.

His mind kept picturing the two of them on the pristine white sheets, making him incredibly clumsy. As soon as they finished, she moved to the door, then stopped.

"I don't have anything for you to wear to bed."

He gave her an uneasy smile. "I don't need anything."

"One of my bulky sweaters might—"

"Joni, I don't wear anything to bed."

"Oh!"

"I'll call Dad first thing in the morning. He's always up about six."

"Good. Maybe he can get here before the rest of the town sees your car."

"Right." And maybe he could get here before Sam broke his promise and carried Joni to bed. Maybe.

Chapter Eight

Joni just barely heard her alarm the next morning, but she automatically thrust out her hand to shut it off.

And found nothing.

Frowning, she struggled to sit up and open her eyes. Not an easy task since she couldn't get to sleep last night. Not with Sam in her bed.

That thought set off an even louder alarm.

Sam in her bed.

Her eyes, seemingly stuck closed a second ago, popped open. She breathed a sigh of relief when she realized she was in Brady's bed, not her own. Where Sam was sleeping.

Her location also explained why she couldn't shut off the alarm. It was in the room next door.

She grabbed her robe at the foot of Brady's bed, pulling it on as she hurried to the kitchen. She sighed as she paused on the threshold. Sam was standing there, his shirttail hanging out, stubble on his face, talking on the phone, and he still looked good.

"What? I can't believe it. How is she?"

Joni's eyes opened even wider and she hurried to Sam's side. "What's wrong?"

He held up his hand to stop her. "Yeah. We'll work out something. Can you come give me a jump, or do I need to call Dusty?"

After a pause, Sam said, "Okay. I'll see you in a few minutes."

"He's coming? Has something happened? Is Brady okay?" Joni asked, bubbling with questions.

"He's coming. Brady's okay," Sam said, answering two of her three questions. Then with a sigh, he added, "A lot has happened."

"What?"

"After we left, Marty called. They'd just gotten word that Paul's father had a heart attack. Mom offered to keep the kids so Marty could go to Denver with Paul. After they dropped the kids off, Mom fell and broke her wrist."

"Oh, no!" Joni said with a gasp. "How is she?"

"She's taking pain pills. Dad said he had to take her to the emergency room last night. He got one of the cowboys to come over and stay until they got back." Sam rubbed a hand over his face.

Joni didn't know what else to say, so she acted instead, making a pot of coffee. She didn't think Sam got much more sleep than she did last night.

Then she took a box of muffin mix and quickly had a filled muffin tin in the oven. Tom wouldn't have had breakfast, either.

Sam had been standing there, watching her, but saying nothing. As she took bacon out of the refrigerator, he finally spoke. "You don't have to do all this, Joni. Go on back to sleep."

"Don't be silly, Sam. You need breakfast, and your dad will, too. Then I'll follow both of you back to the ranch and get Brady. Your mother doesn't need that added complication."

He gave her a wry grin. "You want three for the price of one?"

"You mean Peter and Katie? How long will Marty be gone?"

Sam shrugged his shoulders. "I don't know. She hasn't called yet." With a sigh, he added, "I'd better finish getting dressed before Dad gets here."

Ten minutes later, both men were sitting at her breakfast table.

"This was real thoughtful of you, Joni," Tom said. "I left 'Retta sleeping. I reckon either me or Sam will be doing our cooking for a couple of weeks."

She gave him a sympathetic smile but said nothing.

"You know what was bothering that crazy woman the most?" Tom asked them both.

Sam tried guessing. "Not being able to take a shower?"

"Nope. She hasn't finished wrapping Christmas presents. Now she can't. I told her we'd like the presents whether they were wrapped or not, but she's fretting about that."

"I can understand," Joni said. "Christmas is a big deal, and especially her grandchildren won't understand when things aren't like they expected." She slanted a hesitant glance at Sam, then added, ''I can do the wrapping for her.''

''That's mighty kind of you, Joni. Maybe that will stop her from worrying so.''

Joni doubted it. Loretta played an integral part in the ranch life, she thought. There was a lot to do. But she wasn't going to upset Tom.

She cleaned up after breakfast as the men went out to jump-start the car. Then she dressed, grabbed her hat, gloves and coat and went to the garage, opening the door and starting her car.

Leaving her car running, she walked out to the two men, standing watching the Lincoln's engine run. ''Is it all right?''

''Yeah,'' Sam said. ''But it'll need a new battery. We're going to drop it off at Ronnie's shop in town.''

''Shall I go on out to the ranch?'' If she could find her way.

''Would you mind following Sam and bringing him to the ranch?'' Tom asked. ''I'd like to get back to 'Retta as soon as I can.''

''Of course I will, Tom.''

He surprised her by giving her a hug. Then, after disconnecting the cables, he said goodbye and jumped into his truck.

In seconds, Joni and Sam were standing there alone.

''Guess we'd better get started,'' he said. ''Are you ready?''

''Yes.'' She nodded. ''But I'll have to follow you because I'm not sure where the garage is located.''

"Okay, but stay in your car. They won't be open, and I'm just going to park the car. I'll bring the keys in to them tomorrow."

"Oh. Okay." Again she was reminded that she wasn't in Chicago anymore.

It only took a few minutes to do as he asked. Then, they were on their way to the ranch.

They found Tom in the kitchen, attempting to prepare breakfast for both Loretta and the three children. Joni immediately offered to help.

Tom gratefully accepted. "I guess me and Sam here are spoiled. 'Retta's always taken care of us."

"I'm sure you'll manage," she said.

"I'm going to go check on 'Retta again. Sam, you help Joni, okay?"

Sam stared after his father. "He's still upset."

"I know. Isn't it sweet?" she asked as she finished mixing the biscuits Tom had started.

"Sweet?" Sam asked with a frown.

She couldn't hide the longing in her gaze. But she hoped he wouldn't realize what it was. "The love they share is—is breathtaking. And restores my faith."

Sam stepped closer to her. "You didn't believe in love? But you were married."

"So were you."

"Yeah, but my marriage ended in divorce. I'm supposed to be cynical." He slipped a finger under her chin, forcing her gaze back to him.

"How a marriage ends doesn't necessarily agree with—with what was going on in the marriage." She twisted from his hold and took a cookie sheet out for the biscuits.

He followed her to the counter and leaned his back against it so he could see her face. "Am I to take it from that strange remark that your marriage was unhappy?"

Joni concentrated on rolling out the biscuit dough and cutting perfect circles from it, then placing them on the cookie sheet.

"Joni?"

With a sigh, she stopped and stared at him. "My marriage was—was happy until I got pregnant."

Sam stared at Joni. She was a beautiful woman, with a warm heart. If he loved her—*if,* he reminded himself—and she was carrying his child, he would hold her even closer. Why would her husband react any differently?

"Why?"

She had finished cutting out the biscuits. Setting them aside, she took down a bowl and began breaking eggs for scrambling. "He didn't like not being the center of attention."

He couldn't believe her words. "What are you saying?"

She shrugged one shoulder but said nothing else.

"What did he do? He wasn't abusive, was he?"

"No, other than ignoring me. And ignoring Brady."

He reached out and traced her hair behind one ear, then caressed her cheek. "He must've been crazy," he whispered.

Joni stared at him, tears filling her eyes and her lips, those soft lips, trembling.

Just then the room exploded with the sound of two little boys running into the kitchen.

"Mom!" Brady exclaimed. "What are you doing here?"

"Hi," Peter added. "Where's Grandma?"

Sam replied, "Up to the table, you two, and we'll explain everything."

Joni hugged her son. "Sam, would you pour them both a glass of orange juice? Maybe that will keep them from starving until I've scrambled the eggs."

He poured the juice, then sat down with the boys. "Grandma hurt her arm last night."

"Is she gonna die?" Peter asked, his lip trembling, like Joni's only a moment ago.

"Of course not. But she'll have to wear a cast for a few weeks. And she won't be able to do much cooking."

"Are we going to starve?" Peter asked again, his eyes even wider.

Joni laughed, which did Sam's heart good. She stepped over to the table. "Of course not. Uncle Sam can cook."

"I can?"

"If you get hungry enough," she assured him.

"Eeew," Peter said, frowning. "I want Mama."

Sam and Joni exchanged smiles before they reassured Peter that he was in no danger.

"Oh, I hear Katie," Joni said suddenly. "Breakfast or baby?" she asked Sam.

With a waggle of his eyebrows toward the boys, he said, "Baby."

"Okay, but that means changing her diaper, too," she reminded him.

"No problem," he assured her. As he stood, he couldn't resist kissing her cheek. "Just save me some eggs."

"You want a second breakfast?"

"Yep. Seconds are good." Then he headed for the screaming Katie.

SHE NEEDED TO GO BACK to her little house. To go back to reality. Sam was too much for her to deal with.

Sensitive, caring, supportive. All the things she'd dreamed of in a husband. And hadn't found in her own. She'd adored Derek as a young girl, growing up next to his family. She'd been a foster child. Her foster parents were kind, but she never felt as if she was part of a family.

Next door had been the Evanses. Mrs. Evans opened her home to Joni, talking about always wanting a daughter. Instead she'd had three big, handsome boys. And Joni had fallen for the most handsome, the strongest, the brightest.

She'd thought him perfect.

And he was as long as she believed that, as long as she did whatever he wanted and never complained.

The first morning she'd woken up to morning sickness, unable to cater to her husband's whims, their marriage had begun to fall apart. Gradually he built a life away from home, that didn't include her.

After Brady was born, Joni was glad her husband left them alone. He showed no interest in his son, and Joni refused to abandon Brady to party with Derek.

No, her marriage had not been ideal.

Now she was falling in love with a man who never intended to marry again. So she needed to get away. As soon as possible.

"Mom? Can I have more juice?" Brady asked.

"No, sweetie. I want you to drink milk with your breakfast. I'll pour you both some. Peter, what does Katie usually eat for breakfast? Will scrambled eggs do?"

"Yes, she likes them. Mama feeds her cereal, too. I think Grandma has some in the pantry."

"We'll stick to eggs this morning since they're ready." She poured the milk and put bacon and eggs on the table, along with the biscuits. Sam appeared in the doorway, holding Katie.

He looked like a perfect daddy.

"Um, here, I'll feed Katie," she said, taking the little girl out of his arms. "You sit down and eat."

"I won't argue with those orders," Sam agreed with a grin.

Only seconds later, Tom and Loretta came in, his arm around her in support.

"Loretta! You should've stayed in bed. I was going to fix a tray for you," Joni said.

"Oh, no, you've done so much already, Joni. And

Tom told me about your offer to wrap presents. That is so sweet of you."

"It's nothing. Just helping out like you did when it snowed. Sit down and I'll get you some coffee."

Once they were all settled around the table, silence fell as attention turned to food.

When the boys finished and asked to be excused, Loretta nodded. They scooted from their chairs and raced up the stairs.

"I wish I felt as good as those two," Loretta said with a sigh. "What are we going to do?" she asked her husband.

"About this morning? We're going to stay home," Tom said firmly. "The church won't close its doors because we miss a Sunday."

"I know. But the children—Marty—"

"We'll have to wait until we hear from her. Could be Paul's father is doing great."

"I'll be glad to do anything I can to help," Joni said, unable to resist offering. They were such nice people.

"But you have to work," Loretta said pointedly.

"Yes, but Peter and Katie could go to Mrs. Barker's all day, like Brady. Then I could take them home with me."

"Oh, dear, that would be too much for you to do after teaching all day. I couldn't ask that of you."

"It would only be for a few days, Loretta."

The phone rang, and Tom got up to answer.

Everyone gathered at once that Marty was the

caller, but it was hard to figure out what was going on by Tom's responses.

But Joni noticed that Tom didn't tell his daughter about her mother's accident.

He hung up the phone and returned to the table.

"Well?" Loretta demanded.

"Paul's father is having surgery in the morning, a triple bypass." Tom sighed. "I couldn't tell her about your accident, honey, 'cause she said Paul's mother was falling apart and clinging to her. You know Paul's an only child."

"No, of course you couldn't tell her," Loretta agreed, but Joni could hear the worry in her voice.

"I'll be able to take care of the kids until they get back, really, Loretta." She couldn't stand not offering to help.

"I don't know—could you stay here? I mean, it would be better. We have more room, and I can help some. I just can't do everything. Would you do that for me, Joni?"

Joni heard Sam draw a deep breath. She knew exactly how he felt. Last night they'd spent a miserable time only a few feet from each other. She'd gotten through it by telling herself it was only for one night. Now she was supposed to move into his house and stay for a week?

But she couldn't turn Loretta down.

"I—I suppose we could try it, Loretta. But maybe it would be better if I went home each night and came back early in the morning."

Even Sam joined in protest against that idea. "You'd wear yourself out, Joni."

She stared into his blue eyes. Then sighed and looked away. "You're right. I just hate to impose—"

"Don't you even think of saying that!" Loretta protested. "You're doing us a huge favor. I'll never be able to pay you back."

"She's right, little lady," Tom said even as Joni started to protest. "Me and Sam will help you all we can, but you're saving us."

Sam shoved back his chair. "Why don't I ride with you over to your house to pack. I think Katie will be all right for an hour or two, and the boys are playing. Dad, you help Mom back to bed. Then you can read to Katie or something."

Everyone seemed satisfied with his organization except for Joni. "I want to clean the kitchen first, before I leave."

To her surprise, he accepted her alteration of his plan. Not only accepted, but began helping her, too.

Yep, he was definitely too perfect.

THEY HAD TO CLEAN a second kitchen when they got to Joni's house. The two of them worked in silence. Sam didn't know about Joni, but he was worrying about having her next door to him every night for a week.

He hadn't slept too well last night.

Finally he said, "Are you sure you're all right with this?"

"By 'this' do you mean staying at your parents' house?"

He nodded.

"It won't be—be convenient for the two of us, but I had to offer to help. Your parents are such nice people. And Marty shouldn't have to leave her husband at a time like this when I can help out."

"Hey, I'm grateful you offered. I'm not complaining," he assured her. Only a jerk would think of himself in a situation like this.

"I'll try to keep out of your way."

"Joni, stop. You're going to have me down on my knees begging for forgiveness. You're doing a wonderful thing."

"Thank you."

He remembered what she'd revealed earlier in his kitchen about her marriage. Her husband had been a jerk. Sam wasn't going to make the same mistake.

"You go pack and I'll finish up here," he suggested.

She gave him an uncertain look, then nodded and left the kitchen.

He sighed deeply after she was gone. He was going to have to keep control of his senses this week. Maybe he could convince his dad to spend more time at home while he put in longer hours in the saddle.

That way he'd come in tired, too tired to have any racy thoughts about Joni. He was tired today, too. Real tired. That's probably why he hadn't protested her staying at the house. That and the fact that he hadn't had another solution.

Joni stuck her head in the kitchen. "Are you doing all right? Any questions?"

Her cheeks were flushed and her hair mussed. And he was tired. And he wanted to carry her to that bedroom of hers and make love to her. Man, he was in trouble.

"Fine. I'm almost finished."

"Okay." She disappeared.

He hurried with the cleaning. The sooner they got out of Joni's house, the better off he'd be. At least at home they wouldn't be alone.

When he finished, he called to Joni.

She came down the hall with two suitcases in hand. "I'm ready," she said, her voice breathless.

"Here, I'll take those out to the car, while you check my handiwork and turn off the lights."

He took her keys and opened the trunk. As he was lifting the larger suitcase, Joni locked the front door and came out to the car.

A truck came down the road and braked to a halt beside them, and his friend Dusty rolled down the window.

"Hey, Sam, you two eloping already? Wow, I wasn't even close in the pool. I put my money on Valentine's Day."

Chapter Nine

Though Sam gave an elaborate explanation to his friend, it didn't appear to Joni that he convinced him that they weren't even dating, much less getting married.

She drove without commenting while Sam sat hunched over, resting his head in his hands.

Finally she said, "Surely, when everyone knows about your mother's accident, they'll understand why I'm at your house."

"Of course they will. But that won't eliminate those romance rumors."

"But when we don't marry, they'll die down," she suggested, as she had before.

"But what about Brady?"

"Sam, you're taking your role as Santa Claus too seriously. You can't supply a child with a father just because he wants one."

"What is Santa bringing him? Did you get him a train?"

She rolled her eyes. He wasn't listening to her. She

was the one who would play Santa for Brady. "Yes, I bought him a train. Before we left Chicago."

"The other thing he wanted was a horse." Sam scratched his jaw and stared into the distance.

"No."

"No? He wants a daddy, and you say no. He should have a pony if he's not going to get a daddy."

"Sam! You're being ridiculous. We don't have room for a horse. Not only that, I don't know anything about taking care of one. Do you think Brady does?"

"I could teach him."

Joni gave a gusty sigh and turned into the driveway for the ranch. "He's four, Sam, not fourteen. If I decide we're going to stay here, maybe I'll be able to find a house on a little bit of land. Then we can think about animals."

"I thought you said you liked it here."

It felt as if his blue eyes were drilling holes into her. "I've only been here two weeks, Sam. Everything is going well, but reasons might develop that would make it difficult to stay." Like falling in love with a determined bachelor.

"What reasons?"

"I might develop an allergy to stubborn cowboys!" she snapped, frustrated with him.

His gaze narrowed. "Are you talking about me?"

"If the shoe fits..." She parked the car beside the house. "We'd better get in the house and make sure your parents survived."

"Would you go back to Chicago?"

She stared at the mountains in the distance, the big, blue sky, now that there was no storm. "No."

Her one-word answer seemed to satisfy him. He got out of the car and stood waiting for her to join him.

"I'll check on the kids. You might want to start thinking about what we'll have for lunch," he said with a grin as she came around the car.

"Lunch? It's only nine o'clock. You can't be hungry already."

"I thought we could have lunch at eleven since we won't be in church. Breakfast was early this morning."

"Which one?" she asked, raising an eyebrow.

"The second one was just a snack, to keep everyone company. You're not going to hold that one against me, are you?" he asked with a grin as he took her car keys and opened the trunk.

She shook her head. She couldn't hold anything against him when he smiled that way. It was a good thing she liked to cook, though. She had a sneaky suspicion that would be her main job at the Crawford ranch.

BRADY WAS THRILLED that they were going to spend the week at the ranch, with Peter and Katie.

"You know, Mom, it's like we're a great big family. Isn't it great?"

Tears crowded her eyes and she blinked fiercely. It seemed her craving for a family had been passed on to her son. She wanted to warn him not to lose his heart to the Crawfords, but she couldn't. Why spoil his fun now? It would still hurt if they had to leave.

"Yes, sweetie, it's great. But it'll only last a week."

He beamed at her, but he didn't acknowledge her gentle warning.

"Now, I need some help from you and Peter. I want you both to unpack your clothes, dividing up the drawers. Then figure out what you're wearing to school tomorrow, and lay them out. I'll check your choices later. It's going to be hectic with all three of you going with me. And I can't afford to be late."

With a nod, he raced up the stairs to relay the orders to Peter. Joni sat down with a sheet of paper at the kitchen table and began making a list of what she had to do.

Sam found her there. "You're a list-maker?"

"Not usually, but I think life may be a little complicated this week. If I'm going to be temporary mom, housekeeper and teacher, I'm going to have to be very organized."

"I'm going to try to get Dad to stay here with Mom most of the time. He's not much of a cook, but he can handle the laundry and dusting, waiting on Mom. Things like that."

"I don't think that will be necessary after a day or two. Your mother has to get over the shock, but after that she can take care of herself."

Sam seemed irritated with her response. "We'll see."

"Can you transfer Katie's car seat to my car?"

"Yeah. But you could take one of the trucks."

"I'll be more comfortable in my car."

He studied her, and she wondered what he was thinking. "Okay, but if it snows, or there's even the hint of a storm, you'll take a truck."

"You love to give orders, don't you?" she replied, her chin going up.

Instead of answering, he bent down and kissed her. Then he straightened, just before she reached out to embrace him. "Yeah, especially if it's for your safety."

The difference between this man and her husband suddenly struck Joni. She could trust Sam to make his orders based on what would be best for her and the children. Her husband's orders had only concerned his wants or preferences.

She leaped to her feet. "I need to go make up my bed."

"I'll help."

"No! No, you transfer the car seat."

As she hurried away, he called, "Have you thought about lunch?"

"Pot roast" was her succinct answer. It must have pleased him because she didn't hear any complaints.

THE NOON MEAL was the first time the boys really focused on Loretta's cast. They examined it from every angle and discussed writing their names on it.

"Mrs. Crawford, I saw one with pictures on it, even," Brady explained.

"Dear, you mustn't call me Mrs. Crawford. Why don't you just call me Grandma, like Peter."

Joni shared a stricken gaze with Sam before she tried to intervene. "Oh, I don't think—"

"Okay, Grandma," Brady agreed. Then he looked at Tom. "Can I call you Grandpa?"

"A'course you can, Brady."

"Tom, don't you think other people might think—"

"That we feel like you're family? Probably, but it's the truth, so what's the problem with that?" Tom asked with a warm smile.

Joni couldn't argue with such nice sentiments. She looked to Sam for help. He shrugged his shoulders and said nothing.

"By the way, Joni, this dinner is excellent," Loretta said. "And we can have sandwiches tonight from the leftovers. I don't want you wearing yourself out making meals."

"I enjoy cooking."

"You hear that, Sam? Not like Linda, is she?"

Joni wanted to hide her face under the table.

"No, not at all."

"Who is Linda?" Brady asked.

Peter leaned over. "She was Uncle Sam's mommy, only they didn't have no kids."

"She was my wife," Sam said, correcting him.

"What happened to her?" Brady asked.

Joni sat there, helpless to stop the interrogation, because she didn't know what to say.

"We got divorced," Sam said briefly.

"Oh. That happened a lot in Chicago."

"But you're not in Chicago anymore," Loretta said. "It doesn't happen very often in Saddle. But Linda didn't like it here."

Joni couldn't hold back her question. "But didn't she know Sam would live here? That he worked here?" Her logical mind couldn't accept such delusion.

Tom looked at his son. "Didn't we say she's not like Linda?"

"I got the point, Dad," Sam said sternly.

It was Loretta who answered the question. "She thought she could force Sam to leave. She withheld—"

"Mom!" Sam yelled, getting everyone's attention.

Loretta stopped but she wasn't happy. "Well, she didn't leave any of us in any doubt about what she was doing."

Joni stared at Sam. How awful for him. To have his life's work discarded as if it meant nothing. And to have his wife use sex as a barter for his obedience.

She wanted to reach out and tell him how sorry she was for him, but she couldn't do that. Instead she sent him a warm smile. And said, "Sometimes divorce is the only answer."

Sam looked away and spoke to Brady. "After we clean up the kitchen, how about your mom and I take you boys to the barn. We can pet the horses and I can show you how to take care of them."

"Sam!" Joni protested. The man never gave up.

"Mom, don't you want to see the horses?" Brady asked incredulously.

"Yes, of course, but we'll have to put Katie to bed for her nap, first."

Katie whacked her spoon down on her high chair tray. "No! Me go, too!"

Brady wiped a lump of mashed potato from his forehead. "Girls," he said with a sigh. "They can be such a problem."

The adults laughed, but Joni heard Sam mumble, "I know what you mean."

"Wow," BRADY SAID SOFTLY, standing in front of a large box stall. Inside was a mare and her foal, born only three days before.

"I think he's real beautiful," Peter said, expressing what Brady couldn't seem to say. "Almost as beautiful as my horse."

Brady turned to stare at his friend with even greater awe. "You have a horse? Your very own?"

"Yeah. Santa brought him last Christmas."

All three males turned to stare at Joni, as if Brady's lack of a horse was her fault.

She turned to Peter. "And where do you keep your horse, Peter? In town at your house?"

"No. Grandpa keeps him here for me."

She looked at her son and forced herself to make her point even though it would make him sad. "Too bad we don't have a family member with a ranch, Brady, but we don't."

Her heart swelled with pride when her son accepted

the truth. "I know, Mom. But one day I'll have a horse."

"Maybe Grandpa—" Peter began.

"No, Peter. That's too much to ask. If we stay in Saddle, maybe we'll find a place with a little land," she said, repeating what she'd said to Sam earlier. "And you'll be older, sweetie, and will know how to take care of a horse."

"I have an idea," Sam said quietly, putting a hand on Brady's shoulder.

"What?" Brady and Peter spoke at once.

"We haven't named this little guy," Sam said, gesturing to the colt. "Why don't you help me do that?"

"You mean it?" Brady said, his voice breathless. "You really mean it?"

"I really mean it."

Joni stared at the man, wondering how she could not love him. He was so caring of her little boy, so much more than Brady's daddy had ever been.

"Got any ideas?" Sam asked as he helped Brady climb the rail of the stall so he could see the colt clearly.

"I don't know," Brady said, still awed with the honor. "What do you think, Mom?"

"Well," Joni said, giving the decision all the importance she knew it held in Brady's heart. "He was born at Christmas, so a Christmas name would be nice. How about Noel?"

"That sounds like a girl," Brady said, frowning.

"You could call him Christmas tree," Peter suggested with a giggle.

The two boys began naming everything they could think of connected with Christmas.

When Brady said Christmas cookie, everyone laughed. But he studied the colt, a buckskin like his mother. "That's it!" Brady shouted. "I'll name him Christmas Cookie, and we'll call him Cookie for short. His skin looks just like cookie dough."

"Good enough," Sam agreed with a grin.

"Let's go tell Grandpa and Grandma," Peter suggested, as excited as Brady.

Almost before Joni realized what was happening, the two boys barreled out of the barn, racing across the snow-covered lot to the house—leaving her alone in the barn with Sam.

She cleared her throat. "That was a nice thing you did, Sam. Thank you." She laughed nervously. "And I hope you don't regret your generosity. Christmas Cookie isn't a very elegant name."

He stepped closer. He was wearing his sheepskin coat, hat and boots and looked every inch the rough, tough cowboy.

But Joni knew he had a soft heart.

"Naw, we don't go for the elegant out here. Just whatever fits."

"Well, Cookie is a sweetheart."

"Yeah. So is Brady. And his mom's not too bad, either."

She felt her cheeks redden and took a step back. "Uh, I think I should return to the house. Your mother—"

He took her arm. "Is being well taken care of by

my father. You just cooked a huge meal and cleaned up after it. You deserve a little leisure time.''

"I had a lot of help. You and the boys cleared the table.''

Sam grinned. "I may be a lot of things, Joni, but adept in the kitchen isn't one of them.''

She couldn't hold back a return smile. "But that doesn't stop you from pitching in. I like that.''

"Good. And I like this.'' And he kissed her.

Oh, she liked it, too. His firm lips took control of the kiss. They urged, even pleaded, for her cooperation, and she was quick to give it. Then he lifted his mouth and angled for a deeper kiss, one that sent all thought flying from her mind.

At some point, he must have shucked his gloves because his fingers worked their way beneath her coat and sweater to her skin beneath. "Sam—''

His lips, having inched their way to her neck, flew back to her lips to stop whatever she was going to say. She couldn't remember.

She was filled with a delicious enjoyment of his touch, but it wasn't his touch alone that thrilled her. It was the man himself. His caring ways with her son. His love for his parents. His blue eyes.

She trembled as she realized what she'd refused to admit the past few days. She loved Sam Crawford. She loved the man who had already warned her he never intended to marry. She loved the man who was going to break her heart.

What was she going to do? How could she protect herself?

She grew even more alarmed when he swung her up into his arms, however. "Sam, what are you doing?" she asked, almost groggily, her senses overwhelmed.

"Getting more comfortable."

She understood his meaning when he laid her in some hay, then followed her down. Suddenly her entire body was enveloped in Sam's warmth, his sexiness.

Even as he pushed her sweater up and his lips traced her bra, sending shudders through her, her mind was trying to warn her. But it was a struggle.

And she wanted to kiss his chest.

"Sam, we can't—"

"Yes, we can. Who would come out here on a Sunday afternoon? We're—"

The sound of the barn door opening proved him wrong.

"Sam? Mom?" Brady's voice rang out in the barn.

Sam sprang to his feet, then extended his hand to Joni. She yanked down her sweater, then accepted his assistance to get up. As she hurried by him, she felt his hand in her hair.

"Hay," he muttered.

"Hi, Brady," Joni began, trying to sound nonchalant. "Did you tell— Oh, hi, Tom. I guess you came out to see Cookie." Her cheeks were flaming, but she didn't know anything to do but try to be brazen about it.

"Yeah. 'Retta is sleeping, like Katie, and I thought it wouldn't hurt to step out to the barn." He was grinning like a Cheshire cat at the two of them, as if he had a pretty good idea what they were doing.

Peter stared at them, frowning. "What were you doing in that stall?"

Joni certainly had no explanation.

Sam was silent beside her.

"Oh, I asked Sam to check out the hay. Sometimes it gets old. I imagine Joni was helping him," Tom said glibly enough.

"I guess that's why you have hay on your jeans, Mom," Brady agreed and turned his attention to Cookie.

"Thanks," Sam muttered to his dad, and Joni wanted to add her gratitude, too, but she remained silent. It was too embarrassing, to be caught making out like a couple of teenagers.

Especially with a man who'd already told you he didn't want you.

But he did. She now had no doubt that he wanted her, wanted to make love to her. She'd felt his arousal against her body. And she wanted him.

But their wants were different.

She was stuck here until Marty returned. She'd have to be on her guard every minute, because once he kissed her she was lost.

THE CRAWFORDS HAD A PARTY.

They'd all gotten back to the house a half hour later, after admiring the colt a little longer, when trucks and cars began arriving.

Joni was stunned by the number of people, all bearing food, arriving at the Crawford ranch. Loretta, refreshed from her nap, invited them all in, of course, and immediately asked everyone to dinner.

"Do all these people live nearby?" Joni asked Tom.

"Most. We're not that large a community, but we're all real close. When something happens to someone, we all pitch in. Loretta has been a Trojan about that. She's always taking baby presents, or meals, or running errands for someone."

Joni blinked several times to hold back the moisture that filled her eyes. "That's wonderful."

Tom gave her a quick hug. "You're a country girl at heart, even if you did come from Chicago. Linda, Sam's wife, well, she wouldn't lift a hand for anyone."

"Maybe she didn't understand," Joni suggested, trying to be generous.

"Ha! She understood."

Several more people came in, and Tom moved to greet them, taking Joni with him.

"Howdy, Brad, Steve. Now don't tell me you cooked something," he said, teasing the two men who had entered.

"You're lucky we didn't," the first one said. "But we thought we could offer to help out for a day or two if you need it."

"Thanks, guys. Joni, this is Brad Stover and Steve Bigelow, from the next ranch to the east. This is Joni Evans, a new schoolteacher. She's going to help out with the little ones."

They both greeted her. Then Steve leaned closer. "Your husband here?"

Joni gave a brief smile. "I'm a widow."

Steve's smile widened even as he expressed his regrets. Then he frowned. "You dating Sam?"

"No! Not at all." Her heart hurt with those words, but that was what Sam wanted.

"Glad to hear it. Come on over here and let's get acquainted." He put his arm around her and began urging her toward a sofa.

Sam came back into the room from running an errand for his mother and caught sight of them. Joni expected him to be pleased. After all, she was allowing the cowboy to commandeer her time to satisfy Sam's quest to dispel all the rumors. Her flirting with Steve should take care of that. Of course, she wasn't having to make much effort. Steve was taking care of that aspect.

Whatever she expected, it wasn't the roar that filled the room.

"Get your hands off that woman!"

Chapter Ten

Sam knew he'd made a mistake.

The roomful of people stopped dead in their tracks and stared at him.

Joni's cheeks grew pale, and he was afraid she was going to faint. He took a step toward her and then stopped. What was he going to do? Especially in front of the entire community.

"Uh, sorry, folks. Steve is such a flirt, I thought I should warn Joni," he said with an uneasy smile.

The rest of the audience may have laughed at his words and begun their conversations again, but Steve wasn't buying his little joke. In fact, the cowboy still had his arm around Joni's shoulders and was staring at Sam.

Sam tried to cross the room casually, as if he had no particular destination in mind. But he ended up beside the couple as Steve turned to Joni.

"Well, now, darlin', I thought you said Sam had no claim on you."

"We're friends," Joni said. "I guess he's a little

protective when it comes to cowboy flirts." She made an effort to smile.

"That's right," Sam agreed. "I know how you are with the ladies, Steve. Joni's too innocent to be left alone with you."

"Hell, she's a widow, not some teenager!" Steve protested. "Besides, before you married that—uh, your wife, you had a reputation, too. And soon will again, I suspect."

Sam almost groaned aloud as Joni asked, "What was Sam's reputation?"

"Darlin', there was no one better at mowing down the ladies than Sam here." Steve was quite emphatic.

Joni stared at Sam, as if seeing him for the first time. "Yes, I can imagine."

"Hey," Sam protested. "That was in my younger days."

"Yes, you're so ancient now," Joni agreed softly. Steve laughed.

"You've still got your arm around her," Sam reminded. "I told you to take it off."

"The lady hasn't asked me to remove it," Steve said with a smirk. "Until she does, what you say doesn't matter."

Sam felt betrayed. He glared at both Steve and Joni.

Joni at least recognized the anger building in him. "Maybe it would be best if you unhand me, Steve. I don't want to cause any problems."

"It won't be a problem, darlin'. If me and Sam

come to blows, we'll take it out behind the barn so it won't break up the party,'' Steve assured her.

Sam was ready to head for the barn. He had so much steam rising in him that a release would be welcome.

"No!" Joni protested. "No, that would be absurd. Please release me, Steve. I won't have the two of you fighting, ruining Loretta's party."

Steve, instead of doing as she asked, leaned over and whispered something in Joni's ear. Sam's hands curled into fists.

But Joni eliminated the need for action. She pushed herself away from the cowboy. "You're moving a little too fast for me, Steve. I have a child to raise and—"

"You have a kid?" Steve demanded, his brows suddenly lowered.

"Yes. Brady. He's four years old."

Steve backed away. "Nothing against you, darlin', but I don't mess with ladies with children. I don't want to build a nest. I'm still circling the sky."

Then he disappeared into the kitchen.

Joni laughed awkwardly. "I hadn't realized Brady was a date repellent. I'll have to remember that."

"Only for jerks. Steve's a flirt."

"But he would've served your purpose well. Only you yelled across a crowded room for him to take his hands off me. It was the perfect remedy for your problem. Why did you do that?"

Sam couldn't...or didn't want to explain his actions. But he did want to hold her close, to wipe away that momentary hurt when Steve rejected her because of Brady. And he couldn't do that in front of their company, who, he noted, were still watching them out of the corners of their eyes.

"He's not one to play around with. You'd find yourself in his bed in nothing flat," he muttered, hoping no one would overhear him.

"Do you think I would allow that? I don't fall into just anyone's—" She halted abruptly and her cheeks flamed.

Sam hoped she was remembering how little resistance—none, in fact—she'd given in the barn. He certainly liked remembering it, feeling her soft, warm body beneath his, her arms around his neck, stroking, caressing—

"Hey, Sam!" someone called from the door.

He spun around, prepared to protect Joni again, only to discover his friend Dusty at the door with his fiancée, Lisa.

"Come on, you might as well meet Dusty and Lisa," he said to Joni as he took her hand and tugged her behind him.

After they were introduced, Sam found four chairs together and they all sat down.

"So when are you getting married?" Joni asked.

Lisa eyed her fiancé. "Soon, or the engagement's off."

"Lisa!" Dusty protested.

Lisa smiled at Joni. "Sorry. We've been having this argument all day long."

Joni appeared alarmed, so Sam thought he'd help out. "He told me he was anxious to marry you."

"He was. Until I made a big mistake."

"What are you talking about?" Sam asked.

"Something about giving away the milk before the cow is bought," Lisa said, her voice charged with feeling.

Sam got the inference at once, but it took Joni a minute. "What— Oh." She glared at Dusty, as did Lisa, then, standing, she abruptly said, "Let's go to the kitchen, Lisa."

And the two women disappeared.

"Damn, I didn't expect a public discussion," Dusty complained.

"You idiot," Sam returned. "I thought you loved her."

"I did. I mean, I do. But, well, I need to save money and—"

"And as long as you're getting sex, what's the hurry?"

"I knew you'd understand," Dusty said, relieved.

"Understand, hell! I'm with the ladies. You're being a jerk. She trusted you and now you're betraying her trust." Maybe Sam wouldn't have been so sure about this topic if he hadn't almost made love to Joni. But he knew if Joni trusted him to that point, and he'd promised to marry her, he wouldn't renege on his promise. The pleasure that rose in him at the thought of bedding Joni frightened him, however.

"No!" he burst out.

"No, what? I'm gettin' real confused. Are you telling me I should marry Lisa, or not?"

Sam wiped a hand over his face. He wasn't ready for this—for committing to another woman. For trusting his heart. The timing was wrong.

That was it. Joni was sweet, wonderful—but the timing was wrong.

"Well?" Dusty prodded, drawing Sam back to reality.

"If you love her, and you've already taken her, I think you should marry as soon as possible. What are you waiting for?"

"I told you. I need to save money."

"You've already bought her a ring."

"And that's why I have to save money. I want to take her on a nice honeymoon."

"Did you tell her that's your reason?"

"Of course not. You think I want to admit how little money I have?"

"From what she said, you're going to lose her if you don't explain." He watched his friend. If Dusty loved Lisa, he'd find a way to keep her. If Joni had committed herself to him, he'd do the same.

But she hadn't, of course. The timing was bad.

Dusty leaped up. "I've got to find Lisa."

"Yeah, and I'd hurry, if I were you. Steve Bigelow is here."

Sam followed Dusty into the kitchen. He figured Dusty would drag Lisa off somewhere private, leaving him alone with Joni. He just wanted to protect her from Steve's advances, of course. That was all.

Dusty, however, was too upset. He found Lisa and Joni in the corner of the kitchen, talking. Without any greeting or an attempt to take Lisa somewhere private, he said, "Lisa, sweetheart, the only reason I wanted to postpone the wedding is because I spent most of my money on your ring and I can't afford a honeymoon. But I'll marry you whenever or wherever you say, if you don't mind not having one."

Sam didn't think his friend had drawn breath through his entire speech. That was too bad, because he sure didn't get a chance to breathe with the kiss Lisa planted on him.

Sam decided he and Joni should be the ones to leave, but there was nowhere to go. The kitchen was almost full.

"Oh, Dusty," Lisa said as she broke the kiss. "I just want us to be married. I don't care about any silly old honeymoon." She kissed him again.

Sam discovered Joni had tears in her eyes. His arm slipped around her shoulders and he cuddled her against him. "Hey, don't cry. They're happy."

"I know," she whispered and hurriedly wiped her eyes.

Lisa turned to Sam. "I don't know what you said, but thank you."

"I didn't do anything," Sam quickly assured her.

"I'm glad you're going to be his best man," Lisa said, ignoring Sam's words. "Better get your suit ready."

"Say," Dusty said, beaming with happiness.

"Let's get married on Valentine's Day. Then Sam and Joni could join us and I'd win the pool!"

"The pool?" Joni said, her voice rising. "You mean people are still betting on whether or not—" She broke off to glare at Sam.

"Hey! I haven't bet anything. Don't get mad at me," he protested.

She didn't smile, either. "I thought you would have stopped it by now." Then, she ran out of the kitchen.

"Thanks, Dusty," Sam said in disgust.

"Sorry, buddy. I didn't mean to cause you problems. Especially after you just helped me."

"I'll go talk to her," Lisa said and followed Joni.

"Maybe Lisa can bring her around," Dusty suggested.

"Around to what?" Sam exploded. "I told you there's nothing going on!"

People were staring at him again.

Dusty lowered his voice. "Well, for nothing going on, there's a whole lot of something going on."

Sam sighed. That muddled statement just about summed up his state of mind since Joni's arrival on the scene.

THE CLEANUP wasn't too bad from the party, since some of the guests had brought paper plates and cups. After putting the children to bed, Joni returned to the kitchen.

Even better, as a result of the food gifts, she wouldn't have to cook most of the week. The ladies had brought lasagna, pot roast, chicken salad and more. All kinds of cakes and cookies, too.

She set about making lunches for her and the two boys with the chicken salad. Katie would have jars of baby food. Then she sliced the roast beef and put it in a plastic bag. In another she put sliced tomatoes and shredded lettuce.

That way the men would have no problem making themselves and Loretta a sandwich.

When Tom came into the kitchen, she explained what she had prepared.

"Thanks, Joni. That will make it easy. Of course, we could eat with the hands, but I'd still have to fix something for Loretta."

"Has she gone to bed? Should I bring her some coffee?"

"No need. I'm her personal servant tonight," he assured her with a laugh and a hug.

Sam walked in.

"Uh-oh, I'd better take my hands off you," Tom joked, "or that cowboy is gonna slug me."

Joni blushed bright red and turned away.

"Dad!" Sam protested. "I was—Steve's a flirt."

"He sure is," Tom agreed, still grinning. "But I don't see a brand on Joni, saying she belongs to anyone."

Before Sam could answer, and Joni wasn't sure he intended to, the phone rang.

Tom picked it up. "Marty!"

For the next few minutes, Sam and Joni listened in

to Tom's side of the conversation. It didn't sound as though things were going well.

When Tom hung up the phone, Sam asked, "How is he?"

"He's had some complications. And his wife isn't holding up well at all," Tom admitted. He looked at Joni. "You know, I'm not a women's libber, but I think women should be a little stronger. Marty's having a hard time with her mother-in-law."

Joni smiled at him. "I'm not sure women's lib had all that much to do with it, but I agree. I think every person should be able to take care of him or herself."

"That's right," Tom agreed. "They should all be as strong as you."

Joni blushed. "Well, it may be that she'll grow stronger with time. She's probably in shock."

"Yeah, well, I'll take this coffee upstairs and tell 'Retta about Marty's call." Tom fixed a mug of instant coffee and then headed for the stairs.

Joni began putting everything she'd prepared for tomorrow back into the refrigerator.

"Making lunches?" Sam asked.

"Yes. It's much easier if everything is ready in the morning."

"Were you in shock?"

She looked up, surprised, to find Sam's blue eyes trained on her. "You mean when my husband was shot?"

"Yeah."

She let out a slow sigh. "Yes, of course. You never

expect someone that young to die. And a violent death is always shocking.''

''Did you have someone to help you, support you?''

She didn't want to talk about that time. But Sam stood waiting. ''My foster mother came over. I still talked to her occasionally, and she stayed with me for a couple of hours.''

''What about your husband's parents?''

''His mother didn't handle it well. She sounds like Marty's mother-in-law. I was better off without her around.''

''Your sisters-in-law?''

''They were with Mrs. Evans. It doesn't matter, Sam. I got through it, Brady and I. We're fine.'' She put the last of the food away and faced him. ''I guess I'd better head for bed, so I'll be prepared for the morning.''

''It's not even ten, yet, Joni. Tell me about your foster mother. What happened to your real parents?''

''They were killed in a car accident when I was ten. Too old to be adopted.''

''No family?''

She shook her head. ''Well, there was an elderly aunt, but she wasn't prepared to take on a child.''

''But you weren't abused or anything, were you?''

She fought for a smile, difficult when she thought about those years. ''No, no abuse. But no—never mind.'' She moved toward the door, anxious to end their conversation. He caught her by the arm.

''No what?''

She shook her head, but he didn't let her go. Finally she gave him the answer he wanted. "No love. My foster parents were kind, but I didn't belong to them. I wanted so badly to belong."

She kept her head down, not wanting to see pity in his eyes. That's why he surprised her with an embrace that took the chill out of her body. That lonely little girl in her past absorbed his warmth and felt cared for. Which only made her love him more.

Then the warmth began to sizzle as her body responded to his closeness. Danger.

Apparently Sam recognized the danger, too. He released her and said, "Let's go watch the news. I need to hear a weather report before you start out in the morning."

"Surely we wouldn't have another snowstorm so soon? I mean, don't they—"

"There's no rhyme nor reason to weather, especially in Wyoming. Come on." He grabbed her hand, something that was becoming a habit, and led the way into the den.

Joni wasn't sure that sitting on a couch alone with Sam, even with the weather for company, was a good idea.

"Don't you think you should tell your dad the weather is coming on? He might want to watch it."

"They've got a television in their bedroom."

"Oh."

"Nervous?"

"No, of course not," she lied, tugging her hand from his so she could cross her arms over her chest.

The news portion of the program was just starting when Sam turned on the television. Joni sat as far away as she could without appearing rude and trained her eyes on the screen.

"How do you like our Christmas tree?"

She jumped, shifted her gaze to Sam and then quickly on to the tree. "It's beautiful...and huge. Much larger than the one you cut for us."

"Yeah. We always get a big one. It's a family tradition. Did you have a big one in Chicago?"

"No. Brady didn't know the difference, and it was much easier to get a small one."

"Your husband didn't help with it, did he?" he asked with a frown, as if that fact offended him.

Joni smiled wryly. "No."

"Did he work long hours?"

"Sometimes."

"And the rest of the time?"

"Sam, why are we talking about him? I don't want to."

"I'm trying to understand what kind of a marriage you had, that's all."

"A lousy one. Now, do you want to talk about your marriage?"

"I already told you mine was bad. That's what divorce means."

"Not necessarily. Some people get divorced and remain friends." She was just as curious as he was, but she shouldn't ask questions. The less she knew about Sam Crawford, the less she'd have to remember if she had to go away.

"We didn't. I can't figure out why she married me in the first place. She didn't like anything about me or my life."

"I'm sure she was attracted to you. You're a handsome man."

"Yeah, but not one she wanted to live with. I guess that sounds conceited but—"

"No, I think you'd sound silly denying that you're attractive to women."

"You didn't exactly repel Steve today, either."

"Oh, yes, I did. As soon as I mentioned Brady."

"That's different."

She suddenly realized he'd shifted on the couch, their bodies now almost touching. "Sam, about what occurred in the barn today. It shouldn't have happened. I'd appreciate it if you'd not kiss me anymore."

He reacted as if she'd struck him. "Why?"

"Because I don't indulge in—in making out. I'm an adult, not a teenager with raging hormones." How she hoped he couldn't read her mind, or he'd know she still had raging hormones.

"I don't think a little kissing is making out."

"That's where we were headed, and you know it. I don't want to have to explain myself to Brady."

"Kids see their parents kissing all the time," Sam protested.

"Exactly my point. You are not my husband, or Brady's daddy, and have informed me that you have no intention of being either one."

"Hell," Sam protested, leaping from the couch.

"You're as bad as my parents! Trying to force me into marriage. It's too soon. I don't know that I'll ever want to tie myself down again."

"You think I'm forcing you into marriage?" Outraged, Joni jumped to her feet. "Listen to me, Sam Crawford! I haven't tried to force you into anything except to quit touching me! You don't have the right to maul me whenever you get the urge."

"Maul you? You almost strangled me with your hold around my neck!"

"Well, I can assure you that won't happen again." With that icy return, undermined by her shaking voice, she stomped from the room.

SAM STOOD THERE, wondering when he'd turned into a blithering idiot. He'd just alienated Joni.

Maybe it was for the best. He'd told himself the timing was bad. That he wasn't ready to trust his heart.

But his body wasn't listening.

The urge to touch her whenever she was within sight was leading to some complications. Like the time in the barn. He knew if the boys and his father hadn't come in, he would have had Joni naked beneath him. And loved every minute of it.

Until their lovemaking ended.

Because of the timing.

The time was wrong for commitment, but it sure as hell was right for sex.

Which would put him in the same category as

Dusty when he and Lisa had arrived at the party. Taking his pleasure without paying the price.

He despised men who did that.

So maybe it was a good thing that Joni wouldn't let him near her.

Because he sure as hell couldn't trust his body to back away.

Chapter Eleven

Monday was a long day for Joni.

It shouldn't have been. After all, she had to go to the sitter anyway, but getting all three children in the car, properly dressed, was a challenge. Especially when Katie decided she didn't want to get dressed. Then they'd forgotten their lunches until she had them in the car.

She'd had to leave them alone, with a stern warning about staying in their places, retrieved the lunches and raced back to the car.

At school, the children were all hyper, since this was the last week of school. She'd planned a cutting and pasting activity where the students used tiny squares of colored paper to create a picture of Santa.

As simple as it sounded, the activity turned messy when several little boys glued paper to the nearest girls, and there was a spate of tears as the girls worried about their clothing. When she punished the boys, there were more tears and pleas that she not inform their parents, or even more importantly, Santa.

As a trade-off, Joni made the boys clean the tables

and let the victims be first in line for lunch. After all, it was almost Christmas.

In her spare time, Joni tried to get started on the paperwork necessary for the end of school, since the semester ended before Christmas.

When she got back to Mrs. Barker's, the children were ready to go home. Peter and Katie, in particular, were tired, since they weren't used to day care all day. Katie came running to Joni, whimpering.

"Oh, poor baby, did you have a long day?" Joni asked as she snuggled Katie to her, giving her soft kisses.

"She did fine," Mrs. Barker assured her. "It's just when you came in that she got fussy."

She thanked Mrs. Barker and herded her crowd out to the car. She'd always wanted more children, not wanting Brady to be an only child, but she could see that it would take more energy, or a very supportive husband, to manage a larger family.

Sam would be supportive.

She immediately rejected that ridiculous thought. Sam wasn't even going to marry again, much less help his wife with the children.

When they arrived at the ranch, the boys, after taking their backpacks to their bedroom, as Joni requested, asked to go to the barn, where Loretta had said Tom was working. Making sure they were bundled up well, Joni gave them permission.

"Did everything go well here?" she asked, settling Katie in the den where Loretta was sitting.

"Just fine, except that I didn't get the wash done.

I thought I could manage, but I'm not very good with my left hand. And I don't have much energy. I watched those danged silly soap operas today. Do you know what goes on on those shows?''

Joni grinned at her. ''Yes. Fascinating, aren't they?''

Loretta laughed. ''Yes. I can see how they might be addictive. Do you watch them?''

''No. Actually I prefer books. But during the school year I don't have much time for reading.'' Since she noted Katie was happy with her toys, she asked Loretta to keep an eye on her while Joni put in a load of wash.

When she had dinner almost ready, she walked to the barn to round up the boys and Tom. Her heart was beating overtime in the hope that Sam would be there, too. She'd heard nothing from him since breakfast early that morning.

But he wasn't there.

''Is he still out on the range?'' she asked.

''He said he was going to try to cover the entire fence line on the east meadow,'' Tom said. ''I tried to get him to take one of the hands with him, but he refused. Fixed himself a lunch and hasn't been seen since.''

Joni stared out the barn door at the snow-covered land. ''Aren't you worried?''

Tom shrugged his shoulders. ''Well, maybe. But we'll go to the house and call him.''

''Call him?''

"Yeah, we use cell phones these days. We're 'high-tech,'" Tom said with pride.

Joni was glad, because it meant she'd know Sam was okay in a couple of minutes. She urged everyone to the house, and the phone.

After washing up, Tom called Sam. No answer.

"What does that mean?" Joni asked, sure that some disaster had occurred.

"Probably that he's down in a swallow. A low place," Tom explained. "I'll try again in a minute."

Joni bit her bottom lip and poured milk for the boys. They came running down the stairs, after being sent to wash up, and the three children kept her busy for several minutes.

But she still worried about Sam.

Just before Tom sat down at the table, he went to the phone again. Joni held her breath.

"He'll be all right, honey," Loretta said, patting Joni's hand.

"Oh. Of course. I—I couldn't help worrying—"

"Hey, there. Where are you?" Tom's voice cut through Joni's explanation, grabbing her attention. "Okay. Well, we'll save you some dinner."

"Is he okay?" she asked as soon as Tom hung up the phone.

"Yeah. He said he'd be home in about an hour. That'll be about dark. Dang fool boy tried to do too much. He's a worker, Sam is," Tom said with obvious pride.

"I'm going to be a cowboy when I grow up," Brady informed everyone. "Just like Sam."

Loretta beamed at him. "Good for you. Sam will teach you everything he knows."

Joni bit her lip to keep from saying that they might not be around that long. She'd been worrying all day about staying in Saddle and resisting Sam. Somehow, those two things didn't work well together.

She cleaned up after dinner, but Sam still didn't arrive. Tom offered to help with the dishes, but she asked him to read to the children instead.

When she went into the den, Tom held a sleeping Katie in his lap, with a boy on each side of him. Loretta was dozing in a nearby recliner.

"I'll take Katie up to bed," Joni whispered.

When she came back down, it was time for the boys to be tucked in.

They resisted. "But we haven't seen Sam yet," Brady said pointedly.

"Ranchers work long hours, sweetie. Sam can't always be here, you know. He has things to do."

But Joni knew how Brady felt. She wanted to see Sam, too.

It was more like two hours after dinner when she saw a lonesome cowboy silhouetted against the snow, dragging into the barn. She dropped the curtain and hurried to the kitchen to heat up the lasagna and make a fresh pot of coffee.

SAM SMELLED THE HOT FOOD as soon as he opened the door. How had Joni known he was here? he wondered.

"Wash up. Dinner's ready," Joni said softly as he entered the kitchen.

Since he was hungry down to his frozen toes, he didn't waste time talking. In two minutes he was back at the table, his hat hung on the rack near the door.

Wolfing down the food, he didn't pause until he'd finished and Joni filled his coffee a second time.

"I sure hope this is decaf, 'cause I want to sleep good tonight."

"It is. How about some of Mrs. McGilvey's coconut pie?"

"There's some left over? I won't turn that down. She makes the best coconut pie in the county."

Joni sniffed. "You haven't tasted mine."

Surprised, he stared at her. "You make pies?"

"Of course."

"What kind?"

"Coconut, pecan, all kinds of fruit pies, chocolate."

"Man, whoever marries you will think he's died and gone to heaven," Sam said with a big smile. It slowly faded as he realized he'd offended Joni. Her smiled disappeared and she walked out of the kitchen without a word.

"Damn!" he muttered under his breath.

"You find a rock in that pie?" Tom asked as he came through the door.

"Uh, no. How'd everything go today?"

"Fine. I had an easy day…as you planned."

Sam jerked his gaze to his father. "What?"

"You intended to double your work and halve

mine, but I'd like to remind you that it's your mother who got hurt, not me.''

"I know, but I figured she'd like you close to home until she gets feeling better.'' Sam turned his attention back to the pie.

"Some little boys I know would like to have you come home before their bedtime, too.''

Sam wiped his mouth with a napkin. "I'll go see if they're asleep.''

He slipped past the den without seeing Joni. When he reached the boys' room, he opened the door slowly and tiptoed over to the twin beds. Brady was in the first one, and he stirred.

"Sam,'' he mumbled, "you're home.''

"Yeah, little guy, I'm here. Did you have a good day?''

"Yeah. Grandpa let me pet Cookie and feed him a little hay. It was fun.''

"Good.'' He leaned over and kissed Brady's forehead. "I'll see you in the morning. Good night.''

"G'night.'' Brady shifted, snuggled under the cover, and went back to sleep.

Sam stood there in the shadows, relishing how good it felt to pretend Brady was his. His own son, eager for his daddy to come home.

It was a dangerous delusion.

He backed out of the room, closing the door.

"Were either of them awake?''

He spun around to find Joni staring at him. And this time he saw the weariness in her face. He'd been so hungry earlier, he hadn't noticed.

"Brady kind of woke up. Listen, I didn't thank you for having my food ready so fast. I was starving."

She nodded and turned away.

"Where are you going?"

"To my room. I'm tired. I'm going to read a little and then go to sleep. Six o'clock comes early."

He couldn't think of a reason to stop her. Except that he longed to hold her against him. There was a part of him that was still frozen—and would be until he held her again.

WHILE SAM DID THE READING duties Tuesday night, Joni began organizing the gift-wrapping. Loretta told her where the wrapping paper, scissors and tape were located, and she brought them to the den along with some of the gifts.

"Joni, where did you learn to make bows like that?" Loretta asked after Joni had completed the first present.

Joni smiled. "My foster mother taught me."

"Once I'm able-bodied again, would you teach me?"

"Of course, Loretta."

Joni continued to work, but Sam had stopped reading. Brady elbowed him. "Come on, Sam. Read."

She looked up in time to catch his stare before he turned his attention back to the story.

Even though they'd hardly exchanged a word, Joni was much happier that Sam had made it to dinner. It was alarming how much she depended on seeing him to complete her day.

When Marty returned, Joni would go back to her house, and Sam wouldn't be a part of her day. He might not be a part of her life, if she and Brady left. She'd been giving their departure a lot of thought. She didn't have to get a job right away, since she'd saved almost all the insurance money that came to her with her husband's death. And she received a benefit check every month.

She and Brady could find another small town in Wyoming, with nice people, like those in Saddle. Surely there would be a teaching position open in the fall.

Maybe she would get that land she was talking about, and Brady could have his horse.

A poor substitute for Sam, but the best she could do.

It was a good plan. A workable plan.

But she didn't like it.

Her gaze drifted back to Sam. No, she didn't like the thought of being far from him. Of not seeing him. Not even being able to anticipate seeing him.

He looked up, and she quickly stared at the package again.

When he finished, Brady and Peter spread kisses around the room, then went upstairs with Sam. He came down a few minutes later, reporting that the boys were in bed.

"You're getting good at tucking them in, son," Loretta said with a smile.

"It's easier when there are two of them."

Joni didn't look up. But she grew alarmed as long,

jean-clad legs came to a halt nearby, then folded up as Sam sat down on the floor beside her.

"What can I do to help?"

"Oh, nothing. I'm doing fine."

"Mom, are there other presents to bring down?"

"Yes, but Joni can't wrap all of them tonight. Why don't you go to my closet and get one more stack of boxes. But don't peek in any of them," his mother warned.

After fetching the boxes, Sam gathered up the ones Joni had wrapped and put them under the tree. "I always think a tree looks kind of lonesome without presents under it," he said, staring at the brightly colored packages.

His thought echoed Joni's. "Yes. Though Santa's gifts aren't wrapped, I always pick out a couple of things to put in boxes. But I'm afraid our tree never gets very filled, with just the two of us."

"You'll have more packages under your tree this year, I'm sure," Loretta said with an arch look at her son.

Joni's breath caught at Loretta's inference, that Sam would be buying her a gift. "No, I mean, I don't think—"

Sam helped her out. "I know Peter is already thinking about a gift for his best friend."

She smiled her thanks. "Yes, we've been shopping for Peter and Katie, too."

Tom spoke up. "Sweetheart, I think it's time for you to turn in. You still need to get extra rest." He helped his wife up and led her up the stairs.

Joni, trapped with a pile of gifts still to be wrapped, found herself left alone with Sam.

"I was thinking about a gift for Brady," he said as he passed her the tape she needed.

"You don't need to buy him anything," she hurriedly said.

"Brady and I are friends. I reckon buying him a gift is something I can do if I want."

She gave him a sharp look. "As long as it isn't a horse. We don't have room for a horse."

"Hmm. And what do you want Santa to bring you, Joni? I don't believe you sat on Santa's knee."

That image, her sitting in Sam's lap, took her breath away. After coughing several times, she said, "Nothing. I mean, I want Brady to be happy. That's all."

"Everyone ought to get something for Christmas. Maybe we need to arrange for a private session with Santa."

Joni hoped not. What she wanted Santa couldn't deliver, just as she'd told Brady about his wish for a daddy. And private time with Santa would only make life more difficult.

JONI WENT TO BED before the weather that night. When Sam reached the kitchen the next morning, he said, "You need to take a truck today. They think a cold front might hit us late this afternoon, with snow in it."

Joni didn't want to drive one of the big trucks with

stick shift. She looked out the window. "There's not a cloud in the sky, Sam. I think you're overreacting."

"These fronts can move in fast out here. It'd be safer—"

"If it gets dangerous, I'll take the kids to my house. I need to stop by there anyway."

"Why?" Panic filled him, as if she were planning to leave. That was ridiculous, of course. But he liked having her close.

"I need to check on my plants. Be sure nothing's frozen. Water the Christmas tree."

"Keep a close watch out, okay?"

She nodded and put breakfast on the table.

All day Sam watched the sky. When the clouds, pushed by the Wyoming wind, topped the mountains to the west at about lunchtime, he hurried in and ate his food in front of the television.

The forecaster warned that the storm was building up to be a big one, but he said it wouldn't hit until that evening. Joni and the kids would be back long before that.

He and his dad returned to work, but Sam felt uneasy all afternoon. He told himself it was his food that didn't sit well, but his gaze kept watching the mass of clouds building up. They were about half an hour west of the house when the snow started falling.

Almost at once, his dad's phone rang.

"Okay. We'll be right there."

"What? What's wrong?" Sam demanded.

"Weather forecaster has changed his mind. The full storm will be here in a couple of hours. We've got to get back home." He turned and shouted to his men. Fortunately they were all working together today.

"I'm going to get Joni," Sam yelled, not waiting on the others. He flicked his horse with the reins and rode as fast as he dared on the snow already on the ground. At the house he traded his horse for a truck.

When he reached town, he picked up the kids first.

"What are you doing here, Sam?" Brady asked.

"There's a snowstorm coming, so I thought we should get you home early."

The three kids cheered. Even Sam smiled. He could remember those days. If he was any judge, there wouldn't be any school tomorrow, and they would cheer again.

When he got to the school, he hated to take the three kids out in the snow, but he didn't feel comfortable leaving them in the truck alone.

There were several children still in Joni's room, and she frowned at Sam. "We heard about the storm," she said softly.

"Didn't they let school out early?" he asked.

"Yes, but these two haven't been picked up yet. I can't leave until I'm sure their parents get them." She smiled and shrugged her shoulders.

Sam wanted to sweep her into his arms and ignore her sense of duty. But he couldn't do that. "Mom gave me a list of things to buy at the grocery. Can I leave these three here while I shop?"

"Of course. If my charges leave, I'll load them into my car and—"

"No! Your car is going to stay here. Or at your house if the storm's not too bad. But you're not driving that little car out to the house. It's too dangerous."

"Fine," she said, her voice soothing. "Go do the shopping. Come here, Katie," she said, extending her arms to the little girl.

Sam stared at her, suddenly wishing those arms were extended for him. When she stared at him questioningly, he shook his head and stepped back out into the storm. The coldness, and distance from Joni, helped him think more clearly.

Half an hour later, he returned to find Joni free to go. Together they loaded the children into his truck.

"I'm going to drive my car to the house."

"I'll follow you," Sam replied. "But if you start sliding, we'll park it wherever it lands. I'm not taking chances."

She nodded and hurried to her car. The snow was so thick, he could barely make out the outline, and he wasn't parked far away.

"I can't see Mom," Brady complained as they made their way to Sam's truck. There was a hint of fear in his voice.

"She's getting in her car. We're going to follow right behind her."

"Why can't she ride with us?"

"She wants to leave her car in the garage so it won't freeze up. She'll ride with us to the ranch."

Brady seemed satisfied.

It seemed like hours until they reached Joni's

house. Her car had slid all over the local streets. The plows were out in full force, trying to keep ahead of the storm, but losing the race. The snow was getting deeper and blowing fiercer. Sam realized it was foolish to chance the drive to the ranch—not with the kids in the car. He pulled into the driveway behind Joni. Cutting the engine, he took Katie out of her car seat.

"Are we going in?" Brady asked. The children had been unnaturally quiet on the drive.

"Yeah, buddy, we are. The snow's too thick to make it to the ranch. But we'll all be safe here." And hopefully they would manage to call the ranch before the telephone lines were knocked out.

"Gather up your stuff and be careful. Hold on to each other, boys, because it's deep. We don't want any more broken bones like Grandma."

With Katie tucked inside his jacket, they made their way to the front porch and he banged on the door.

Joni opened it almost immediately and helped them inside, taking Katie from Sam. "What's the matter. Do we need a bathroom break?" she asked, her voice anxious.

"Nope. We have to take a storm break. We can't make it to the ranch. If you don't mind, we'll be spending the night here."

Her eyes widened. "Of course. That's fine. Uh, boys, take your things to Brady's room." She watched them leave the room. Then she turned to face Sam again. "There's only one problem. We only have two beds for five people."

Chapter Twelve

"We'll manage," Sam assured her. "I can sleep on the floor, if need be. Right now I need to call Mom and let her know we're safe."

"Oh. Of course. The phone's in the kitchen."

The two boys came running back down the hall.

"Mom," Brady called. "Me and Peter can't fit in my bed. We're too big."

Joni wasn't surprised. Brady's bed was not even twin size. He'd had it since he moved out of the crib. "Um, I guess the two of you had better take my bed, and we'll put Katie in yours."

"But where will you and Sam sleep?"

Good question. She stared at the small sofa in the living room. She could fit on it, but Sam was much too big. But he was her guest. She couldn't put him on the floor while she took the sofa.

"I got through to Mom," Sam announced as he came back into the living room.

"Oh, good. Are they all right?"

"Yeah. Do you have any wood for the fireplace?"

Joni hadn't had a fire in the fireplace since they arrived. "I haven't used it. Are you cold?"

"No, but if the electricity goes, it will get very cold. I'll see if there's any wood in the garage or on the back porch." He walked out before Joni could get out any words.

Shock held her silent. Electricity goes? Did he mean they would be without heat? She stared out the front window at the white rage that was coating the world in snow.

"Mom, are we going to freeze to death?" Brady asked, his eyes wide.

She shook her head. "No, of course not. We'll be just fine. We, um, need to get organized. You can share a pair of your pajamas with Peter. Katie can wear one of your long-sleeved shirts and a pair of socks."

"What's Sam going to wear?"

Brady's question almost distracted her from their situation. The thought of the long, lean cowboy in white cotton briefs, assuming he wore that much, made her mouth go dry.

Sam's arrival rescued her from her paralysis. He was covered with snow, clutching a load of wood to his chest. "I think there's enough wood on the back porch."

"Hey, Sam, you're a snowman!" Brady exclaimed, chuckling.

"That's right and you'd better keep your distance or I'll melt on you," he returned with a smile.

"Boys, take Katie to Brady's room and play with her while I help Sam," Joni ordered.

"I can bring in the wood," he protested.

"I thought I'd bring in the things you bought at the store," she said. As the children left the room, she added, "And I'm praying diapers were on the list."

Sam grinned. "Your prayers were answered."

"Thank you," she muttered with a relieved sigh.

"But I'll get the groceries after I bring in the rest of the wood," he assured her.

"Don't go all macho on me, Sam. It's already getting dark." She was pulling on her coat even as she spoke. When she turned toward the front door, he grabbed her arm. Irritated that he would try to stop her, she spun around, ready to tell him what she thought of macho men who counted women helpless.

Instead of protesting, Sam kissed her. As he lifted his lips from hers, leaving her reeling, he murmured, "Be careful." Then he turned and headed for the back porch.

She stared after him, stunned by his kiss, until the children's laughter awakened her. "Oh, yeah," she responded when he couldn't hear her. She'd be careful.

The force of the storm struck her as soon as she stepped out the front door. By the time she'd made two trips to get all the groceries, she was frozen and exhausted.

Sam met her at the door on her second trip, taking the packages from her at once. "Any more?"

"No, that's the last of them."

"Go sit down by the fire and I'll put these things away," he ordered.

For once she didn't protest. It was nice to have someone want to take care of her. Even temporarily.

When Sam came back to the living room, he carried a cup of hot tea for her.

"How thoughtful of you, Sam. Thanks." She sipped the hot liquid, feeling it seep through her frozen body. "Oh, that tastes good." She studied the pile of wood Sam had put on the hearth. "Do we have enough wood? Should we be using it already, while the electricity is still on?"

"I think we have enough. And I've only made a small fire so we'll be ready. Do you have any candles?"

She set down her cup and headed for the kitchen. Once she'd rounded up what candles she had, she decided to start dinner. "I don't want to cook over an open fire. I've never done that before."

"I have. I'll become cook if the electricity goes," Sam assured her.

"Gee, it might be worth doing without electricity to see you cook over the fireplace," she teased with a grin.

"Yeah, and I could wear one of those aprons that say 'Kiss the Cook.' Or you could," Sam said softly and came closer.

"I've got to make dinner," she said breathlessly. "Go check on the children." After a look that seared her insides, he walked out of the room.

She leaned against the kitchen counter, waving her hand in front of her face. She thought there had been a sudden heat wave named Sam. Who needed a fireplace?

WITH EXQUISITE TIMING, the electricity went out just as they finished dinner. Sam took the children upstairs to dress for bed while Joni did a quick cleanup in the kitchen by candlelight.

When she went hunting for the rest of them, she discovered them all in the living room, with a few adjustments. The mattresses from both beds were on the floor in front of the Christmas tree.

"Look, Mom. We're going to have a slumber party," Brady announced as she entered.

"Yes, I see." She looked at Sam. "We're all going to sleep in here?"

"Yeah. By keeping the doors closed and the fire going, we'll be pretty warm."

"Unless we have to go to the bathroom," Brady whispered.

"Yeah," Peter added, "and the water's real cold."

"Ah. Thanks for the warning."

"You'd better go change while the bedrooms have a little warmth left," Sam suggested. "The kids have changed."

Yes, she could see that. Katie was wearing a pair of Brady's thick socks that came all the way to her diaper, topped by a long-sleeve knit shirt. The boys both wore flannel pajamas and thick socks.

"I don't have anything for you to wear, Sam," Joni said, frowning.

"I'll sleep in what I've got on. Don't worry about it."

A few minutes later, she returned to the living room, dressed in an old pair of sweats and thick socks, carrying all the bedding she had. Sam had all the kids sitting in front of the fire, leaning against him, telling them a story. Katie, snuggled in her uncle's arms, was already drifting off.

When she reached for the little girl, Sam said, "Put her on the sofa."

"She'll fall off," Joni warned.

"Use a chair to block the edges."

She did as he asked, but where they would all sleep occupied her mind while Sam finished the story. They sat quietly, seemingly mesmerized by the snapping, crackling fire.

Then Peter tugged on his uncle's sleeve. "Uncle Sam, are my mommy and daddy all right?"

"Sure they are, Pete. They're down in Denver. It's probably not even snowing there. Besides, you know your daddy will take care of your mommy. That's what daddies do."

"My daddy didn't," Brady said abruptly.

"Brady!" Joni exclaimed with a gasp, stunned by her son's words.

"He didn't, Mom. I remember he made you cry."

Joni wanted to crawl under something to hide her embarrassment. To her surprise, it was Sam, with his arm around her son, who came to her rescue.

"Well, Brady, all we men mess up sometimes and make our ladies cry. But we try to make up for it. Your daddy may not have had time to do that before he was shot. That means you've got to remember to apologize if you do something wrong."

"I will, Sam," Brady promised solemnly.

Joni stared at the fire, barely able to deal with the emotions that flooded her. For the first time since her son was born, someone else dealt with a problem.

Sam's words hadn't taken long. But they'd been a tremendous help to Joni. He'd given respect back to Brady for his father. Whether her husband deserved it or not wasn't important. Brady needed it.

She turned her head to discover Sam watching her. Though her lips trembled, she gave him a grateful smile.

"Time for bed, boys," Sam said, giving each of them a hug.

"But where are we going to sleep? My bed is too small for both of us," Brady assured Sam.

"Naw, it's not. The closer you are to each other, the warmer you'll be."

"Are you and Mom going to sleep on the other mattress?" Brady asked even as he and Peter jumped onto his mattress.

"Yeah. We're going to keep each other warm, too," Sam said casually, not even looking at Joni.

She couldn't breathe.

Was the man crazy?

She stared at him until he asked her if she intended to kiss the boys good-night. "Oh! Yes, of course."

She scooted over to the mattress and hugged each boy, warning them to be quiet in the morning if Katie was still sleeping.

Then she returned to sit in front of the fire, her back to Sam.

Maybe she'd stay there all night.

WHEN SAM CAME BACK into the living room after his turn in the bathroom, he discovered Joni still staring at the fire burning brightly, her back rigid.

He picked up several more logs to add to the fire before sitting beside her. "You all right?"

"No, I'm not." Her voice was more frozen than the world outside.

"Did I overstep my bounds, talking to Brady about his daddy?"

She faced him, her cheeks red, all stiffness gone. "No! Not at all. In fact, I appreciate what you said. I—I didn't know what to tell him."

Sam grinned back, glad she'd forgotten to be angry. "No problem. From what I've heard about your husband, he wasn't worth much, but Brady doesn't have to know that."

They sat silently, watching the fire. Then Sam added, "Whatever I think about your husband, I have to give him partial credit for a great kid." He noted moisture in Joni's eyes and decided it was time to tease her again. "And fine taste in women."

She immediately fired up, as he'd known she would. "Sam Crawford! You are an awful flirt!"

"Can't help myself, Joni," he assured her. "You're too much for a man to resist."

"Well, you'll just have to work harder at it. And for your information, we're not going to share that mattress."

"We have to, Joni. In spite of what I said earlier, I'm too old to sleep on the floor, and we need each other to keep warm. I promise to behave."

"You?" she questioned, clearly doubting his promise.

"Hey, I keep my word. Besides, we have too many chaperones for me to try anything," he admitted ruefully.

She sighed, then nodded. "Will Katie be all right sleeping by herself?"

"Yeah, she's snoozing just like the boys. Come on. Let's get tucked in." In spite of himself, his pulses began racing at the thought of holding Joni in his arms.

"What if the fire dies out?"

"It won't. I'm going to sleep on the side by the fireplace so I can replenish it during the night." He sat on that side of the mattress and removed his boots.

"Are you going to be comfortable in your jeans?"

"Are you asking me to take 'em off?" He cocked one eyebrow at her.

"No!" Her cheeks were bright red and he wanted to warm his hands there. "I—I was worried about—never mind!" She slid under the covers and turned her back to him.

He blew out the candles and joined her in the bed.

As soon as he stretched, he reached for her, pulling her back against his chest.

"What are you doing?" she gasped.

"We're not going to keep warm if we cling to the edges, Joni. Just relax and get some sleep. I bet the kids will be up early."

She held herself taut for several minutes before she capitulated, her body sinking against his.

Heaven.

And hell.

"SAM?"

The whisper barely penetrated Sam's head as he snuggled against Joni. When it was repeated, he struggled to open his eyes.

"Hi, Brady," he muttered. "What's up?"

"The fire's almost out. Should I put some more wood on it?"

Reluctantly Sam withdrew from Joni and slid from under the covers, the difference in temperature considerable. Last night he'd lectured the boys about not touching the fire. He didn't want to go back on that order.

"I'll do it. Thanks for wakening me."

Brady hovered nearby while Sam built up the fire.

"Get on this end of the couch and I'll put a blanket over you."

Brady did as he ordered but the boy kept his eyes on him. "Are you leaving?"

"Nope. I'm going to the bathroom, then I'll see what I can find for breakfast."

When he returned a few minutes later, Sam had a pan with water in it that he sat on coals, some granola bars and two cups, one with instant cocoa, the other instant coffee.

As soon as their drinks were ready, he scooted under the cover with Brady.

"Why did you wake up so early?" he whispered to Brady.

"Peter kicked me in the stomach. He rolls around a lot while he sleeps."

Sam smiled. "Yeah, I forgot about that. He's kicked me before, too."

"Does Mom kick?"

Sam's gaze strayed to Joni, curled up under the cover. She hadn't kept him awake by kicking. But her sexy body had done a number on his attempts to sleep. "Uh, no. I didn't sleep because—because I was worried about Dad doing the chores by himself this morning."

"It's still snowing."

"I know."

"If we were at the ranch, I'd help you with the chores. Will Grandpa be able to feed Cookie?"

"You bet."

They sat in silence for several minutes, and Sam drank the coffee, hoping the caffeine kicked in soon.

"Sam?"

"Yeah, Brady?"

"I wish you were my daddy instead of my real daddy."

His arm tightened around the little boy.

"Is that bad?" Brady asked anxiously.

"Not bad, no. If I had a little boy, I'd want him to be just like you. But—but I'm not ready—I can't get married right now." He must have built up the fire too much. He was sweating.

"Why not?"

He looked down into Brady's anxious eyes, warm brown just like his mother's, and tried to come up with an answer the boy would understand. "Marriage is serious business. I've already messed up once. I can't marry again until I'm sure it's forever."

Brady tucked his chin into his chest. "Oh."

"Your mom's a pretty lady. She'll find lots of guys who would like—I mean, you'll have a family again. Just be patient."

"But not you," Brady said sadly.

"Brady—"

"You're up early, son," Joni said, sitting up suddenly in bed. "Couldn't you sleep?"

"No, Peter kicks," Brady said succinctly.

Joni looked at Sam, her gaze cold, before she turned back to Brady. "Sorry, sweetie. Sometimes life is like that."

Sam didn't think she was talking about sleeping with Peter.

"Why don't you come help me check the kitchen? There might be something there for breakfast," she said as she rolled out of bed, stretching out her hand for Brady.

"We've already found some granola bars," Sam protested even as Brady left him.

She shot him another cold look and led Brady out of the room without speaking.

Sam had the feeling she'd overheard all their conversation.

"ARE YOU MAD AT ME for getting up early?" Brady asked as Joni stared at the pantry shelves.

"Of course not," she assured him, stooping down to give him a hug. "How about oatmeal? It's nice and warm, and I have some raisins to go in it."

"I like oatmeal."

"Why don't you go get the pan from the fire and bring it to me? And don't burn yourself."

He ran out of the kitchen and she leaned against the doorjamb, letting out a long breath. She'd heard Brady when he first whispered to Sam, so she'd been privy to all their conversation. She'd wanted to cry at Brady's sad response.

Instead she'd vowed that she would take her son away from Saddle, away from the man he wanted as a daddy. Away from heartbreak.

She couldn't do anything about it until the snow-storm disappeared, but she would as soon as she could. She'd been holding out against a move, hoping things would work out.

But she couldn't do that any longer. Brady was already too fond of Sam.

The door swung open and she straightened. But it wasn't Brady carrying the pan. It was Sam.

"I told Brady to—"

"I was afraid he'd burn himself."

She couldn't argue because he protected her son. She reached out for the pan.

"I'll take care of it. You want more water heated?" Sam asked, watching her.

"Yes, please. We're going to make oatmeal." She turned her back on him to take the oatmeal from the pantry.

"How much did you hear?"

She turned to face him even as he filled the pan. "Everything."

"I tried to be honest," he said defensively.

"Oh, you were brilliantly honest." She gave the package of oatmeal a savage rip, trying to release her anger.

"I didn't want to hurt him."

It wasn't easy to hide the heartbreak. But she did. After all, it wasn't Sam's fault that both of them fell in love with him.

"What are you going to do?"

She wouldn't tell him she was leaving. Not yet. "I'm going to do what I should've done in the first place. I'm going to keep my distance from now on. No more of your misguided attempts to fool everyone. We're going cold turkey, Sam Crawford. Turkey as cold as a Wyoming blizzard."

Chapter Thirteen

It was hard to be aloof when you were trapped in one room with the object of your aloofness.

That was a truth Joni discovered as the day progressed. She tried to avoid conversation with Sam, but with three children under their care, even talking couldn't be avoided.

But her quietness didn't disturb Brady. In fact, he seemed in agreement with her. Frequently, while Sam played with his nephew and niece, Brady sat quietly by his mother, watching.

"Don't you want to play with us, Brady?" Sam asked, frowning. He'd been on all fours chasing Katie and fighting off Peter who pretended Sam was a bucking bronc.

"No, thanks. I'm helping Mom," the boy said. In actuality, he was holding the mending basket with thread and extra needles while Joni repaired some of his clothes.

"And I appreciate it," she said with a hug.

Sam eyed the two of them, as if they were keeping a secret from him. "Well, I was kind of hoping you'd pick out your favorite storybook, so I can rest while I read it to the three of you.''

Brady couldn't resist that lure. He slid from the sofa and made a mad dash to his bedroom, hurrying back before he got cold. ''This is it,'' he said, handing a much read *Peter Pan* to Sam.

''Aha!'' Sam said with a grin. ''Are you never going to grow up, like Peter Pan?''

''Yeah!'' Peter yelled.

Brady, who in the past had expressed such feelings, looked first at Sam and then his mother. ''I don't know.''

Joni smiled at her little boy, knowing he was growing up before her very eyes. She wished it wasn't so painful.

Sam, too, seemed to realize Brady was having difficulties. Scooping him up in his arms, Sam sat on the sofa. ''Don't worry. You've got time.'' Then he motioned to Katie, toddling toward them. ''Come on, baby. You, too, Peter. We're going to read.''

About one o'clock, the phone rang. When Joni answered, she discovered Loretta on the line. ''Loretta! How's everything out at the ranch?''

''Fine. Marty called. They're in Cheyenne tonight and will be home tomorrow.''

''That's wonderful. How's Paul's dad?''

''Doing much better. How are my grandkids?''

''Fine. I'll let you talk to Sam.''

She called Sam to the telephone and went back into the warm living room to tell Peter and Katie that their parents would be home tomorrow.

When Sam came in a few minutes later it was to announce that the snowplows were out again. They could go back to the ranch within the hour.

Peter cheered and Katie followed suit, though Joni doubted that she knew why she was cheering. Brady looked at his mother.

"No, sweetie, we won't be going with them," she said softly.

He didn't say anything, as if resigned.

"What are you talking about?" Sam demanded.

"I was explaining to Brady that we won't be going back to the ranch with you. Since Marty and Paul will be back tomorrow, I'm sure your mother can manage until they arrive."

"They have a generator at the ranch. You can't stay here without electricity." He sounded in charge, as always.

Joni ignored him. "I think we have enough time for cookies and milk. Anyone interested?"

Katie's favorite word, cookie, always got a reaction from her. Brady and Peter also accepted the offer, though not as enthusiastically. They were whispering between them.

When Sam tried to follow her to the kitchen, she reminded him he had to keep an eye on Katie around the fire.

But he hadn't gone away when she returned with a tray of milk and cookies. Taking it from her, he poured Katie her roly-poly glass of milk, and glasses for the boys. Then he faced Joni, his hands on his hips.

"I'm not leaving you and Brady here without electricity. And I don't want any argument."

He was a formidable foe, his aggressive stance emphasizing his muscle and determination. But Joni wasn't going to back down. "Brady and I are staying here."

"Why?"

"Because Brady has been hurt enough."

He opened his mouth, then closed it again. He reached out and held her arms. "I'll go stay in the bunkhouse, but—"

"And how would you explain that to your folks? We'll be fine and you know it. There's still plenty of wood left. We'll be at school again tomorrow, I'm sure. We'll be fine."

"Joni, I don't think—"

"Aren't you gonna have cookies and milk, Uncle Sam?" Peter asked, interrupting them.

Joni sagged in relief when, after staring at her, Sam turned to Peter and joined the tea party.

JONI AND BRADY stood on the front porch and watched as Sam's big truck drove slowly away, following the tracks of the snowplow.

"Will they make it all right?" Brady asked in a small voice.

"Yes, sweetie. You know Sam's a good driver."

He looked up at her. "He's good at everything."

Her smile wobbled a little but she held on to it. "I'm sure there's something that Sam's not good at, but I can't think of what it is right now." She squeezed Brady's shoulder. "Let's go inside and figure out what we're having for supper."

After they'd eaten, the two of them sat on the end of Joni's mattress and watched the fire burning.

"I like having a fire," Brady said.

"Yes, it's good company, isn't it?"

"Yeah. Are we going to stay here, Mom?"

Trust her son to cut straight to the important stuff. She didn't know what to say. "I'm not sure. Why don't we wait until after Christmas. We'll talk about what we'll do then. I think we ought to enjoy Christmas first."

"Yeah," he agreed with a sigh, and laid his head on her shoulder.

IT WAS A RELIEF to return to the normalcy of school, even if the day wasn't normal. The children were so excited, she could scarcely keep them in the room. There wasn't much work done, but at least they had no more gluing incidents.

In fact, each child had made a gift for Joni, making her feel so welcome, tears filled her eyes. When the bell rang, instead of their wild rush from the room, each child gave her a hug, thanking her for coming to teach them.

When the last child left the room, she slumped in her chair, glad she would have two weeks to recover. And decide what she intended to do. Could she and Brady be happy in Saddle without Sam in their lives?

Mary stepped to her door. "All gone? Were they as wild as mine?"

"I suspect so."

"Are you going to the church party this evening?"

They'd announced the event when she'd visited the singles class, but she hadn't thought of it again. "I had forgotten all about it. Besides, I'm not a member of the church yet."

"That doesn't matter. You're still invited. Besides, I was hoping you would go."

Joni stared at Mary's disappointed face. "Why? Are you going?"

"Usually I don't, but I thought—well, I wanted to go to see Donald again."

"Hasn't he asked you out?" From their enjoyment of each other last Saturday night, Joni assumed they were now a couple.

"We went out for pizza on Monday night, but he's been so busy with the storm, animals getting hurt and all, that I haven't even heard from him. I thought I might see him at the party tonight. Every single in town usually goes."

"And you wanted us to go together?" Joni asked.

"Well, I figured you might be going with Sam, but just in case you weren't—" Mary broke off, her cheeks flushed.

Joni hadn't planned to go, but if Mary was right, her not going with Sam would make an impression. And she wanted Mary's romance to succeed, even if hers didn't.

"If I can find someone to keep an eye on Brady, I'll go with you, Mary. But I won't know until later. I'll have to call you."

"Okay," Mary agreed eagerly.

"Um, what do I wear? I mean, what kind of party is it?"

"Oh, it's wonderful. We all pile on a bed of hay, pulled by Mr. Wilks's big horses, and we go to several nearby ranches to carol. Then we come back to the church and have hot chocolate and visit. So dress warmly."

"Okay. I'll call you."

After Mary left, Joni leaned back in her chair and sighed. She hadn't wanted to go out this evening. But if she had any hope of staying here, and she wasn't sure she did, she had to find a life without Sam.

And she had to convince the town there was no connection between the two of them.

When she reached Mrs. Barker's, she asked the lady about keeping Brady that night, but the woman already had plans. She gave Joni the names of some possible sitters, but she also passed on a message from Marty, Peter's mother, asking Joni to call.

At home, it seemed strange to be there without Sam and the other two children, but Joni reminded herself that they had only moved in three weeks ago. It would take a while to feel at home. And at least the electricity was back on.

Brady moped into his room, and Joni picked up the phone to call Marty. When she answered, Joni asked about her in-laws and the drive back. Then Marty thanked her for all the help she'd given the Crawford family.

"I also wanted to ask if Brady could come spend

the night. You deserve some time off, and Peter missed Brady all day long.''

"Oh, Marty, you don't want an extra after all you've been through."

"Peter is so much happier when Brady is here. It will be easier on me, Joni, I swear."

"Are you doing this because Sam asked you to? Because of the church party?" she asked.

"Oh, no, I forgot all about the singles party. Everyone in town goes. But no, I haven't even seen Sam today. Are you going?"

"Well, Mary wanted me to go with her, but I didn't have a sitter."

"Don't give it another thought. Bring Brady over right now, so you'll have plenty of time to get ready. But why aren't you going with Sam?"

"Sam and I aren't dating, Marty. He's just been a friend," Joni hurriedly explained.

"Well, whoever you're going with, bring Brady over. Peter will be leaping for joy when I tell him."

"Thanks, Marty. I will." She took down directions and, after hanging up, walked to her son's bedroom door. He was slumped on his bed, staring at the ceiling.

"Feeling kind of down?" she asked.

"Yeah. I miss Peter and Katie, and Grandma and Grandpa. And most of all I miss Sam. And Cookie."

Joni knew just what he meant. Their house seemed small and empty. "Well, I can't take care of all those problems, but Peter's mother called and asked if you could come spend the night. Would that make up for some of them?''

Brady shot off his bed as if fired from a cannon. "Yeah! Can I, Mom? Can I?''

Joni smiled at the change in her little boy. "I suppose so, if you promise to mind your manners.''

"I gotta pack a bag,'' Brady announced, diving into his closet for the overnight bag he used to visit the ranch. "Peter wants to play my new video game. And I should take my G.I. Joe. He has one, too. And—''

"How about some pajamas and clean clothes for tomorrow? I think they should go in there, too.''

With Brady's suddenly energetic assistance, Joni had him ready to go in about ten minutes. She drove him to Peter's house, chatted with Marty a few minutes, then returned home.

After calling Mary, who insisted she would pick Joni up, Joni indulged in a hot bubble bath. Normally she didn't even try since her son found several emergencies that needed her personal attention anytime she did.

As she lay in the hot water, surrounded by sweet-smelling bubbles, she considered her situation. She'd already admitted to herself that she'd fallen in love with Sam. Not only was he handsome, sexy, intelligent and charming, but he was also sweet to Brady. Caring, fatherly. But the timing was wrong. She knew he wasn't interested in forming a family.

So, she had to establish a separate identity from the sexy Santa she'd met on that first day. Tonight was the first step. She would make friends with the other singles in town. Already she was becoming friends with Mary.

Maybe she'd even flirt a little. Just a little. Sam's idea of her dating someone else was a good one. As long as she didn't let anyone get serious about her. Because, if there was no pressure on Sam, he might one day realize how perfect they would be, the three of them.

She swirled her hand through the evaporating bubbles. Was she misleading herself? Was there no hope? She didn't think so. She knew Sam was attracted to her. And she knew he cared about Brady.

All she needed was patience.

And distance.

Okay, so she had a plan of action.

Tonight she would socialize.

SAM GOT BACK TO THE HOUSE after dark. He'd planned to come in early, but he'd found several head of cattle trapped in a deep snowdrift and had worked for the last three hours to free them. He was frozen and exhausted.

The electricity had been restored that afternoon, his mother told him as he came in.

"Then I'm heading for a hot shower. It's the only way I'll get warm."

Tom, already in the kitchen, said, "Your mother and I will have you some hot food ready when you get out."

Sam had just walked back into the kitchen when

the phone rang. Tom answered, then held out the receiver to Sam.

"Hello?"

"Sam? This is Donald. Are you picking up Mary as well as Joni for the party?"

The party. Sam had forgotten all about the church party while he worked that day. "Damn! I forgot all about it. We haven't made plans. Why?"

"Well, I got back late and—well, I'd forgotten to say anything to Mary about it and when I called, there was no one home."

"Just a minute." He covered the receiver with his hand. "Have you talked to Joni today?" he asked his mother.

"No. Marty did."

"Did she say anything about going to the party?"

"The singles party?" Loretta asked. Sam thought she was pretending innocence and nodded impatiently. "Why yes, she did. Marty is baby-sitting Brady so Joni can go."

"Alone?" Sam demanded.

"I think she's going with Mary."

He turned back to the phone. "Mom says Joni and Mary are going together."

"They won't be alone for long, with all the guys. You know they always outnumber the women. I've got to hurry."

"I'll swing by and pick you up. No sense in having too many cars there."

"Good thinking. When will you be here?"

Sam eyed the food on the table hungrily. "In about fifteen minutes."

Loretta began making him a roast beef sandwich before he'd even hung up the phone. He raced back upstairs to put on a warmer shirt and came back down. "Thanks, Mom," he said as he grabbed the sandwich, stuck a soda into his coat pocket, put his hat on his head and ran for his truck.

"Good thing that boy has no interest in Joni," Tom said with a big grin. "Otherwise he might've had to forgo his dinner to get there in time."

"I know," Loretta said with a smile. "Isn't it wonderful?"

EVERYONE ARRIVING for the party met in the room they used on Sunday morning. When Mary and Joni walked in, there were already more than a dozen people present. Though normally shy, Mary felt an obligation to introduce Joni, and they both found themselves talking to several of the men.

However, neither Donald nor Sam was present.

That was a good thing, Joni hurriedly assured herself. Of course, not for Mary. Mary seemed to have fallen for Donald and wanted to see him again.

At least Donald seemed open to the idea of dating. Mary was lucky.

Billy, the man she'd met at the pizza parlor, walked in. When he saw Joni, he came over at once.

"Hey, Joni, how are you?" he greeted her, a smile on his face. "Where's Sam?"

Joni seized the opportunity to demonstrate her singleness. "Sam? I wouldn't know."

Brad, a well-built cowboy who had a cocky grin, moved a little closer. "I heard you and Sam were an item."

Joni smiled. She wasn't impressed with him. He would be terrible father material. But as a way to establish her availability, he was perfect. "No, not at all. Actually I'm friends with his sister. So he's helped me out occasionally."

Brad wasn't buying her story yet. "Sam's not one to pass up a pretty face."

"Thank you for the compliment. But I think you've forgotten that Sam just got divorced. Sometimes it takes a man a while to be interested again."

Several people nodded agreement, and Brad stepped a little closer. "How about I help you stay warm while we're riding in the hay?" he offered.

Joni wasn't ready to move quite that fast. "I brought a blanket to keep me warm. But I wouldn't mind the company."

Brad grinned and offered her his arm. "My pleasure. Have you ever been on a hayride before?"

Joni laid her hand on his arm, but she didn't feel anything. Why should she? Only Sam seemed to evoke that response from her.

"Why, no, they don't have a lot of hayrides in Chicago. Will you show me what I'm supposed to do?" She batted her lashes as she smiled.

"Oh, darlin', before we get back tonight, you're

going to learn a lot," he assured her amid the laughter of those around him.

"Don't forget, Brad," one man called out, "this is a *church* social. You gotta behave yourself."

Brad smirked at his friend and said nothing, but Joni knew the man had no intention of behaving.

But she was a big girl. She could take care of herself.

When they reached the parking lot, she saw the large flatbed trailer covered with a mound of fresh hay. The horses attached to it were Clydesdales. "Oh, I want to look at the horses. They're magnificent," she exclaimed.

"Sure thing," Brad agreed, leading her to them. "They're friendly. Go ahead, pet them."

She rubbed the velvety nose of the closest one, telling him how pretty he was. Before she moved to the others, Mary called out to her.

"Come on, Joni. They're going to help us up."

She returned to her friend's side, closely followed by Brad. One of the men was already up on the trailer, and they had placed a small stepladder next to it. Mary climbed to its top step and took the man's hand. Joni followed her as Mary settled in the hay on the blanket she'd brought.

Brad put an arm around Joni. "You don't need to let someone else help you up. I'll do it."

She didn't want to be too encouraging. "That's all right." She stepped to the ladder. The man beside it took her arm as she climbed to the top step. Then the man on top reached down for her hand. As he pulled her, and her blanket, to the top of the trailer, a truck screeched to a halt in the parking lot.

Chapter Fourteen

"Isn't that Joni?" Donald said, peering through the windshield as Sam brought his truck to a stop.

He threw the truck into Park and scrambled out. "Come on, before they leave us behind."

In all, almost twenty-five people were gathered for the caroling, and Sam and Donald were the last ones to climb aboard. They discovered their quarries surrounded by a number of men known to be unattached.

"Make room," Sam calmly ordered. "I need to share Joni's blanket because I forgot my own."

Brad didn't move. "Sorry. Joni offered to share with me."

Sam glared at Joni, sitting next to Brad.

While she didn't welcome him with a big smile, she did lift a corner of the blanket. "I think there's enough for three of us."

Sam insinuated himself in a space on the other side of her, unhappy that Brad was there. But at least he was next to her, too.

"I didn't know you'd decided to come," he whispered in her ear as the horses started their stately gait. The trailer creaked along behind them.

"Mary wanted me to come with her," she returned before answering a question Brad had asked.

Before there was more conversation, the leader of the group began passing out music for their caroling.

"Did everyone bring a flashlight? I have a couple of spares available if you didn't."

Joni pulled a flashlight out of her purse. Mary had warned her to bring one. "Did either of you bring—" Joni began, then stopped. The two men were busy glaring at each other and didn't seem to care about the music.

"What are you doing here, Sam?" Brad demanded in a low growl. "I heard you were too heartbroken about your divorce to be interested in the social scene."

"Who told you that?" Sam growled back.

Brad nodded his head in Joni's direction and she chewed her bottom lip at Sam's angry stare.

"Brad asked if you and I were dating. I thought I should explain why we weren't."

"After all, you don't usually pass up a pretty lady," Brad added.

"Just because I'm not ready for—for a commitment doesn't mean I don't enjoy a lady's company."

"Most ladies like to know there's a future in a relationship," Brad said.

"Then why would they ever go out with you?" Sam demanded.

Feeling she was sitting in the center of a war zone,

Joni wrapped her blanket around her and scooted several feet away, bumping into Donald.

"Hey!" Sam protested.

"Where are you going?" Brad demanded.

"Away from you two. I don't sense a lot of Christmas spirit between you." She smiled at Donald. "Hi. How are you? Mary said you've been busy with a lot of customers."

"Mary said that? Is she angry with me?"

"Why don't you go ask her?" Sam suggested, shifting closer to Joni again.

"Sam!" Joni protested.

What was wrong with her? She wasn't interested in Donald, was she? She hadn't acted upset last Saturday when Donald had devoted himself to Mary.

Donald looked longingly at Mary but made no move to get closer.

"You know," Joni said softly, "Mary came with me. Not any of those men. And she was hoping to see you."

"But there's no room over there."

Sam gave a disgusted sigh.

Joni patted the vet's arm. "After we stop to carol at the first house, maybe you'll have a chance to sit beside her when we get back on the trailer."

Since Brad had followed Joni to sit beside her too, the three men surrounded her. Sam hoped she was happy. But she'd encouraged Brad, so it was her fault he was there. And she's the one who moved to Donald's side.

So their unmatched foursome was her fault.

After all, he was only there to protect her.

JONI DECIDED MEN were crazy.

When they reached the first ranch house near town, they all climbed down from the truck and formed a loose semicircle in the front yard. Sam and Brad each maintained their positions, beside her.

Donald, however, seemed to recognize his opportunity. He moved through the crowd until he reached Mary's side. Her welcoming smile must have convinced him she was glad to see him. His arm went around her and they stared into each other's eyes.

Joni was happy for them. She was glad that at least one romance was going well. Because hers certainly wasn't.

She glared over her shoulder at Sam. What was the man trying to do? It had been his idea that she show interest in another man. He wanted off the hook. He'd told her time and time again that he wasn't interested in a future with her. So why was he clinging to her now?

They began to sing "Joy to the World." Joni joined in the singing, trying to remember why she was here tonight, in addition to making people believe she and Sam weren't dating. She was here to celebrate Christmas with her neighbors, to sing Christmas carols as a gift to others.

"Think they've got the hang of it?" Sam asked, a half smile on his lips, nodding in Donald and Mary's direction.

She looked at him, then away. "Yes, I think so. At least Donald knows what he wants."

"Do you?"

His whispered question shook her. Of course she did. But she also knew it was impossible. She turned to Brad, determined to shut Sam out of her life. "You have a beautiful voice."

"Thank you. I'll serenade you anytime you want."

She smiled but said nothing. The man responded to mild encouragement like a love-starved old maid. When they finished the song, the leader announced their next song would be "Silent Night," Joni's favorite Christmas carol.

It was easy to believe in a silent night, long ago, especially away from the busy, noisy city streets of Chicago.

Wrapped up in the music, she scarcely noticed when Sam's arm went around her shoulders. His baritone voice joined with hers and, for Joni, the choir became one of two people, her and Sam.

"Look up at the stars," he whispered in her ear.

She did as he said, stunned by the beauty of the night. It was hard to believe that twenty-four hours ago, they'd been trapped by a blizzard. Now, shiny stars numbered in the millions, it seemed, twinkling in the crisp, cold air.

Sam chuckled. "Mom used to tell us those were God's Christmas tree lights."

"And you believed her?" Joni asked, her voice husky.

"Yeah, until I noticed they were still there a month later." He tightened his arm around her.

The carolers began "O Holy Night" and they joined in.

As she lifted her voice in song, Joni didn't think she'd ever experienced such a wonderful celebration of Christmas. She wished Brady were here to experience it.

As if he read her mind, Sam said, "Too bad Brady isn't here to see it. Kids need to know there's more to Christmas than Santa Claus."

A round of applause interrupted them, letting them know the caroling was over for this house, and the other singers were moving back to the wagon.

Joni told herself she was glad they were interrupted. It was too easy to fall under Sam's spell.

She hurried over to the driver of the large horses. "May I share the seat with you so I can see how you drive the horses?"

He stared at her. "Well, I reckon, if you're sure you want to. Seems to me there's lots of fellows who would be more interesting company."

She beamed at him. "Not at all. I can't wait."

He led her to the trailer and showed her how to reach the driver's seat. By the time Sam reached the wagon, she was already in place.

Sam, however, wasn't so easily dismissed. "Hey, Bill, would you let me drive the team for a while?"

"Ain't you got better things to do?" Bill asked, but there was a smile on his face.

"Nope."

"Well, come on. You can drive to the next stop."

Before Joni could protest, Bill climbed onto the hay, leaving his seat for Sam.

When he settled down beside her, she protested. "What are you doing? How are you going to convince everyone that we're not dating if you stay at my side?"

"I thought you rejected that plan," he said mildly, gathering the reins.

"Not exactly," she said with a shake of her head. "But it wasn't working. I thought if I came to the party without you, people would realize—and it would've worked, too, if you hadn't acted like Brad was trespassing!" she snapped.

"He's a dangerous flirt."

"Another one?" she asked incredulously. "This county must be full of them."

"Just Steve and Brad. You seem to attract them."

"I must, since you're included in that group."

"Hey! I'm not a flirt."

"Ready to start!" someone shouted and Sam gathered the reins, slapping the horses on their backs.

Joni actually did enjoy watching Sam handle the reins. As with his truck, he seemed in complete control of the majestic animals. And the jingle bells attached to the harnesses rang through the night air, reminding her of childhood dreams of Santa.

"Brady would love the bells."

"Yeah, he would. He'd probably want to decorate Cookie with bells."

They drove in silence, and Joni felt isolated with

the man she loved. In the darkness of the cold night, lit by a full moon and the twinkling stars, she could almost pretend her problems were solved. That Sam loved her as she loved him, and that he wanted to be a family with her and Brady.

Almost.

Desperate for something to distract her from her dangerous thoughts, she studied his large hands as they managed the reins.

"Is it difficult?" she asked.

"Managing the horses? Not these. They're well trained." He looked at her. "Want to try?"

"Would it be all right?" she asked, thrilled at the idea.

"Sure. Here, hold them like this," he said, offering the reins to her. As she tried to imitate his grasp, he looped his arm around her, pulling her against him.

"What are you doing?"

"Helping you, that's all." Since his right hand, the one that had snaked around her, grasped her hand and helped her hold the reins, she couldn't dispute his claim.

"You can feel them pulling the load," she exclaimed, beaming at Sam.

He dropped a kiss on her lips.

"Hey, no kissing while you're driving," someone called amid a burst of laughter.

Joni was horrified. "Sam, my plan is never going to work if you keep doing things like that."

"And your plan is what?"

"The same as yours. To show people we're not a

couple. You're the one who thought it was so important."

"I know. But I've been thinking."

She held her breath. Had he decided he was interested in a future with her and Brady?

"What?"

"You're widowed. I'm divorced. We're both used to, uh, certain things. I'm not ready for a commitment yet, but I think we should, uh, explore the possibilities. I mean, who knows what the future will bring?"

Joni's heart ached and she slapped the reins back into his hands, inadvertently signaling the horses to go faster.

"Oh!" she gasped, grabbing the seat as the horses picked up their pace.

Sam, with his arm still around her, eased back on the reins, settling the horses into their steady gait.

As soon as he'd done so, Joni tried to duck beneath his arm, so she wasn't in his embrace any longer.

He lifted his arm, making her escape easier.

"Hey, what's going on up there?" someone called.

"Amateur driver," Sam shouted back. He drove silently for several minutes before he looked at her again.

Joni stared straight ahead.

"Did I upset you?"

"Yes."

"I'm trying to be honest, Joni. You know I'm attracted to you. Physically we're well suited. I'm just suggesting we let our relationship follow its natural path. Who knows, we may not be physically compatible.''

She almost burst into laughter. And would have if her heart hadn't hurt so much. "I don't think there's much hope of that."

"Maybe not. But it wouldn't hurt anything. We'd be taking our relationship to the next level. It happens every day."

"We're not even dating, Sam," Joni said pointedly. "That's what I was trying to prove tonight."

"But we both know that's not true, Joni. We're connected, even if we're not following the normal pattern of two people who are interested in each other. You just agreed that we share an attraction."

"You're right, I can't deny that," she agreed in a low voice.

Sam pulled the horses to a stop, and she panicked, afraid of what he might do. Her control was fragile.

"Easy. We're at the next house," he said in a low voice.

He swung down from the seat on the opposite side of the trailer from where the others were unloading and held up his arms to Joni. After hesitating, she climbed down. Halfway, he pulled her into his arms. Before she could protest, his mouth covered hers, and she experienced the blankness she had before as her senses went into overdrive.

Her arms circled his neck, and the cold night air heated up. His hands slid beneath her coat, stroking her back. One hand sank to cup her bottom, pulling her tighter against him. She was left in no doubt that he was aroused.

Which only increased her need.

He lifted his lips and reslanted them to go deeper, to bring them closer. She did her best to accommodate him.

"Hey!" Brad shouted.

She and Sam broke apart to discover the cowboy staring at them.

"Sorry," Joni began.

Sam was less diplomatic. "Mind your own business, Brad. Joni and I had some private discussion to take care of."

"Yeah, I saw what kind of discussing you were doing. What about your ex-wife?"

"What about her?" Sam challenged, taking a step forward.

Joni took the opportunity to slip around him and head for the group getting ready to sing. She only hoped the two men would be sensible.

Because she couldn't make sense out of anything right now.

SAM REMAINED BY HER SIDE the rest of the evening. As their voices blended in Christmas carols, his warmth wrapped her in a fantasy that promised as much hope and love as the holiday itself.

On the hay wagon, he held her close, stealing the occasional kiss. There was no conversation. Sam seemed to realize she needed time to think.

And the evening was as convincing as he was. In

the pure night air, it was easy to believe that tomorrow would be as magical, as wonderful as being held in Sam's arms.

Even the hay beneath them reminded her of that moment in the barn, with Sam beside her, his hands caressing her, driving her to heights she'd never reached before. She didn't think she'd ever smell the scent of hay without thinking of Sam.

Sam leaned even closer. "You thinking?"

She nodded but didn't speak. His words, however, pushed her to consider the most serious part of his plan.

Brady.

As much as she loved Sam, and that love appeared to be growing every day, she loved her son more. And Brady was her responsibility. She had to think how her and Sam's relationship would affect her little boy.

If Sam were committed to family, to the three of them, she'd have no hesitation at all. He'd be the perfect father for Brady. And Brady would be ecstatic.

But his offer to date, to explore their attraction, to make love wasn't the same thing. And it could lead Brady to believe that it was.

And break his heart.

SAM HELD JONI against him in the dark, loving the warmth of her that spread through him. He wanted to try to persuade her to let them grow closer. But he wanted her to come to him willingly, not because he'd overwhelmed her.

He still had difficulty with the thought of remarrying, but he also had difficulty with the thought of walking away. He needed time, but he also needed Joni.

He figured in six months he would have worked out his problems. By then, he and Joni would have shared a lot of intimacy, an idea that made his heart beat faster. And he and Brady would be even better friends.

A lot of couples anticipated their wedding vows. Dusty and Lisa had. Of course they were engaged, but that didn't make that much difference, did it?

An uneasiness filled him. Maybe he was lying to himself, being unfair to Joni. He'd told Dusty he should go ahead and marry Lisa. Sam snuggled a little closer to Joni, as if afraid she'd be torn from his arms. Damn it, he needed her!

But he'd have to wait for her to decide. He wasn't going to force her into a corner. He couldn't when he—he closed his eyes. He panicked as he realized he'd been about to admit to loving her. No. He cared about her. That was it. He cared about her.

And that was the first step to loving her, of course. Which made him feel good. When he was ready for commitment again, it would be to Joni. But the timing was wrong.

Damn it, the timing was wrong.

When the hayride ended, Sam led Joni to his truck, still holding her close, wrapped in the magic of their warmth. Neither spoke on the short drive to her house.

Sam eyed its silent emptiness with appreciation. He loved Brady, but he didn't need the boy here tonight.

By the time he'd gotten out of the truck and reached Joni's side, she was already standing in the snow. He took her arm and hurried her up the sidewalk.

Tonight he was going to satisfy the hunger that filled him whenever he touched this woman.

As they reached the porch, he couldn't wait. Pulling her into his arms, he kissed her with all the desire that filled him.

And she responded.

Anticipation built and he took the keys from her hand. "Come on, sweetheart, let's go inside," he suggested, longing for the comfort of bed…and a naked Joni.

She pulled away from him and took her keys back into her grasp. Then she looked up at him.

"No."

Chapter Fifteen

"No?" Sam replied, pain filling the one word.

Joni stood rigid, avoiding his stare. "No," she repeated. "I'm—I'm not ready."

Sam eased his hold on her, and tilted up her chin. "Damn, sweetheart, if either of us were any more ready, we'd be naked in the snow."

She bowed her head, resting her forehead against his broad chest. "I have to think, Sam. And I can't do that around you."

"It doesn't require any thought, sweetheart. Just let your body do the talking. I'll take care of you."

"There's too much involved. I—I have to think of Brady. I want to be sure I'm doing the right thing." She pulled away from him. "I have to go in."

He was frustrated. She didn't have to look at him to know that fact. She recognized it in herself. But she had to be sure.

As she walked to the door, he finally spoke. "Fine. You know where to find me if you change your mind."

She slipped inside before she could change her

mind right then. And leaned against the door until she heard the roar of his big truck disappearing down the road.

Then she quickly undressed and got into bed, curling into a little ball of indecision. What was she going to do? She wanted to make love with Sam. But she wanted their union, their loving, to be something to celebrate, something on which to build a future.

She had a lot of thinking to do.

The next several days, she could scarcely function. Brady frequently complained about his mom's distraction.

"Mom, are you listening?"

"Yes, dear," she muttered, cleaning the kitchen after breakfast on Tuesday.

"What are we gonna get Sam for Christmas?"

Her cheeks flamed. She knew what Sam wanted.

"We're going to get him a present, aren't we?"

Yesterday, they had shopped for presents for Peter and Katie. And in the afternoon, they'd baked cookies to fix a plate for Marty and Paul. Tomorrow, she intended to bake a special Christmas cake for Tom and Loretta.

But Sam?

"I—I don't know. I guess we can go shopping. Or we could give him a plate of cookies." Her fingers were shaking. The man was driving her crazy.

"I don't want to give him cookies. I want to buy him something," Brady said, his brow furrowed in thought.

"How about a nice pair of leather gloves. He has

a pair to work in, but I don't think he has a pair to wear to church.''

That was the least personal gift she could think of that Sam might use.

''How do we know if they'll fit?''

''We'll call Loretta and ask her. She'll keep the secret,'' Joni assured her son.

''Okay. But tell her not to tell Sam.''

Relieved that they'd settled on something so easily, Joni reached for the phone.

Once she'd explained her reason for calling, Loretta not only told her what size but where she should shop for the gloves.

''Thanks, Loretta.''

''We've missed the two of you,'' Loretta said as Joni prepared to hang up.

Joni cleared her throat, trying to ease the tightness she felt there. ''Um, we enjoyed staying with you. How are you managing?''

''Okay, though cooking is definitely difficult.''

''May Brady and I come see you tomorrow afternoon? We're going to make a special cake for you, so you won't have to worry about having something for Christmas.''

''Joni, you are the sweetest person. Plan on staying for dinner.''

''No, we can't, Loretta, but thanks for asking. We'll come about two o'clock. Have to go, thanks for the advice,'' she added before hanging up the receiver.

"You didn't tell her not to tell Sam," Brady said urgently, his gaze full of concern.

"Sweetie, Loretta knows it's a gift. She won't tell Sam." Joni hoped she wouldn't mention their going to the ranch, either. She needed to avoid Sam.

LATER THAT AFTERNOON Joni and Brady bundled up and headed for the store Loretta had recommended. Joni hadn't visited it before, because she hadn't had all that much time for shopping.

Brady had no interest in looking around. He immediately went to the gloves section.

"Well, howdy, young man. Can I help you?" an old man asked.

"Yes, I need to buy gloves."

"These are men's gloves. The ones for you—"

"No, it's a gift. For a man."

"Ah, buying your daddy a Christmas present?" the man asked with a smile.

Joni cringed.

"No, he's not my daddy. But I wish he was." Brady turned heart-filled eyes to Joni.

She ignored his blatant hint. "Choose which gloves you think he'll like, Brady."

Brady began looking at the several styles and colors, but he seemed unable to make a decision.

"Maybe if you tell me something about him, I can help you," the man said.

Joni sucked in a deep breath.

"Sam's a cowboy," Brady began, "but we're buying gloves for him to wear to church."

"Sam? Sam Crawford?"

"Yeah. Do you know him?"

"I sure do. And I know just what he'd like." The man handed a pair of black leather gloves to Brady, then smiled at Joni. "Sam's a good man."

She didn't need to be told that. She needed to avoid adding to the rumors. "We're friends. He's—he's been very helpful."

"I heard. You must be Joni Evans."

The man extended his hand, and Joni shook it, but she wished she'd never entered the store.

"I like these, Mom. Can we buy them for Sam?"

"Yes, of course, you can give them to Sam." She looked at the man who had introduced himself as the owner of the store when they shook hands. "Brady wanted to buy Sam a present because he considers him a friend."

"He let me name one of his horses," Brady said, his little chest puffed out with pride.

"And what name did you give it?" the man asked as he wrapped the gloves in tissue and put them in a box.

"Christmas Cookie, 'cause he's the color of cookie dough."

The man chuckled. "Good choice." He told Joni the amount she owed and rang up the sale after she'd paid him.

"If these don't fit Sam, you tell him to bring them back to me and I'll fix him up," he said as Joni took Brady's hand and headed for the door.

It was a nice store, but she wouldn't be back anytime soon.

JONI STARED AT HER IMAGE in the bathroom mirror. She was going to have to make a decision. Otherwise she'd look like an old hag and Sam wouldn't be interested.

The dark circles under her eyes were the result of not sleeping again last night. Because she wanted Sam. How could she not want him? She loved him with all her heart. She ached for him.

But she feared putting Brady's heart at risk.

Her only hope was that Sam would come to need her as much as she needed him. Did men grow dependent when they were intimate with someone, like women did?

She didn't have the answer to that question, but she did know that she couldn't continue as she had.

With Brady's help, she carefully made the cake for Loretta and Tom. It was in the shape of a Christmas tree, and they spread green icing on it, adding M&M's for Christmas ornaments.

"Grandpa and Grandma are going to love this cake!" Brady exclaimed.

"I'm sure they will," Joni said. She'd bought a pretty Christmas platter as part of the gift.

"When are we going?"

"I told Loretta we'd be there about two."

"Then are we going to Peter's house to deliver his and Katie's presents?"

"I suppose we might as well. But, Brady, they may

not have presents for you, so don't get your feelings hurt, or expect anything.''

Brady grinned at his mother but said nothing. She suspected he and Peter had already discussed the present situation, but she couldn't be sure.

The doorbell rang and Joni's heart double-clutched. Then she calmed herself. It wouldn't be Sam. After all, it was the middle of the day and he'd be working outdoors.

But she didn't realize how much she'd hoped it was him until she opened the door and said hello to the postman. Depression filled her.

"Got a big package for Joni and Brady Evans," the man announced cheerfully. "Here, let me set it inside for you. It's kind of heavy.''

"Thank you," Joni said, then asked him to wait. She returned with a plastic bag of Christmas cookies.

"Why, thank you. Those are my favorites. Merry Christmas.''

After the door closed, she turned to her son. "Look, Brady, a package from Grandma and Grandpa Evans. Let's open it.''

"Okay," Brady said, no excitement in his voice, "but we have to hurry 'cause we're going out to the ranch.''

The boxes inside the large one were individually wrapped. She let Brady choose one to open early. He picked the largest, discovering a toy gas station with cars.

He frowned. "Cowboys don't work at gas stations.''

"Yes, but cowboys drive cars and trucks and go to gas stations."

"That's true. Me and Peter can pretend we're hauling hay, or picking up a new horse, and we have to stop and buy gas."

"Right." In Brady's head, everything centered around cowboys now. And she knew whom to thank for that fascination.

"Is it time to go to the ranch? I want to tell Sam about my gas station."

"We have to eat lunch first."

"Grandma will have something to eat. She won't mind."

Joni sighed. "Brady, she might, but it's impolite to invite yourself to a meal. And you must remember she's not your grandmother."

Brady scowled and kicked the big box.

"Put the rest of the presents under the tree while I fix us some lunch."

She escaped to the kitchen, but she couldn't escape her thoughts. Their lives seemed to revolve around Sam Crawford, like a moon circling a planet. She stared into space, thinking of Sam, until Brady came to the kitchen.

"Where's lunch?"

SAM CAME IN TO LUNCH a frustrated man. He couldn't forget Friday night and the feel of Joni in his arms. He couldn't forget her answer.

She'd ask for time.

Hell, how much time did she need?

She'd had five days. He'd counted every one. Every lonely one.

He missed touching her, talking to her, seeing her. Damn it, he missed Brady, too.

"Hurry and get washed up, Sam," Loretta called. "I'm going to need some help."

His mother was doing fairly well. She'd gone back to the doctor Monday and had her wrist X-rayed. He'd put on a small cast, that left her fingers free. But some things were still difficult for her.

When he came into the kitchen, his father was helping her put food on the table.

"Looks good," he remembered to say, for his mother's sake.

"*Humph!* The way you've been eating, you'd think I've forgotten how to cook," Loretta complained.

Sam felt his cheeks redden. Okay, so he'd been off his feed a little. There was no need to make a big deal about it.

"Hasn't been sleeping well, either," Tom added.

"How do you know?" Sam demanded. "I haven't bothered you."

"Nope. But you've got such big bags beneath your eyes, I thought maybe you'd packed all your belongings and was leaving." Tom grinned, daring his son to contradict him.

"Cute, Dad, real cute," he returned in disgust. It wasn't nice to make fun of his discomfort.

He only hoped they didn't know what was going on. Because if they heard what he had in mind, he figured they'd be angry with him. They treated Joni as if she were a daughter.

He filled his plate, then pushed the food around with his fork, his mind turning back to Joni and whether or not she'd ever speak to him again.

"Sam! Eat! With everyone coming this afternoon, I want you to help me clean the kitchen before you go back to work."

He frowned. "Everyone? What are you talking about?"

"Marty and the children are coming out this afternoon to bring some presents. And Joni and Brady are bringing us a Christmas cake."

"Joni and Bra—Joni's coming here?" he asked, leaping to his feet.

"Yes, at two," Loretta said calmly, staring at her son. "Sit down and eat your lunch."

Sam sat down, his mind racing. Joni was coming to the ranch. She must have made a decision. She wouldn't come if she didn't want to see him, would she?

"Did she ask about me?"

"No, dear, she didn't. Well, I take that back. There was one question but—"

"What? What did she ask?"

"Brady had a question about your Christmas present."

His eyebrows almost met in the center of his face, he frowned so fiercely. That wasn't the answer he wanted. He wanted Joni to ask about him. To—

"You do have a present for Brady, don't you?"

Tom asked. "Your mother and I found a sheepskin coat just like yours. We thought that would make him happy."

"Yeah." In fact, he had two presents for Brady. A plastic horse with all the gear he could put on and take off. Sam figured Brady could learn about horses with it. And a cowboy hat, a real Stetson. Just like his.

They were going to look like twins.

Or father and son.

Not what he'd offered Joni. Not yet.

"Do you have a present for Joni?" Loretta asked.

He nodded and said nothing else. He'd visited the only jewelry store in town on Monday and bought a diamond-and-ruby drop necklace for her.

He hoped she didn't throw it back in his face.

"Well, eat up. We need to get the kitchen straightened."

Sam followed his mother's orders. When they finished cleaning the kitchen, it was only one-thirty.

His father kissed his mother's cheek, picked up his hat and headed for the door.

"You coming, son?"

"Uh, I need to, uh, there's something, uh, I think I'll wait to say hello to Brady."

Tom grinned and nodded. "Good idea. Say hello for me, too."

MARTY AND THE KIDS arrived first. "Sam, what are you doing in the house? I thought you'd be working."

"Uh, I wanted to see you and the kids," he muttered, bending to kiss her cheek.

"How sweet of you," she said in disbelieving tones and then looked at her mother.

Sam saw Loretta's quick shake of the head, indicating Marty shouldn't ask any more questions. That was okay with him, as long as his mother didn't say anything.

"Hi, Uncle Sam," Peter said, catching his hand. "We've got presents in the car."

"Terrific. Want me to carry them in?"

"Yeah, and I'll help. I'll show you which ones 'cause we have things for Brady and his mom, too."

Sam looked at his mother. "You haven't told them?"

"Why, no, I forgot to mention that Brady and Joni are coming by this afternoon."

Marty smiled. "Oh, that explains—"

"She's bringing us a Christmas cake," Loretta hurriedly added, interrupting Marty's words.

Marty continued to grin, but she didn't say anything embarrassing. "Then, Peter, you and Uncle Sam can bring in all the presents. You can give Brady his present when he and his mom arrive."

Sam grabbed his nephew's hand and headed outside, leaving the two women whispering.

"I've missed Brady. We're like brothers," Peter said.

"Yeah, he's a great friend."

"Mommy said even if you and Joni got married,

he wouldn't be my brother. But wouldn't he, kind of?"

"He—he'd be your cousin. That's almost a brother."

"Great!" Peter exclaimed as Sam opened the door to the car.

"Peter, Joni and I aren't— I mean, she's a friend."

"Oh."

They heard the sound of an engine coming closer.

"I bet that's Brady!" Peter shouted.

Sam saw the car in the distance. Yeah, that would be Joni. His "friend" was certainly making his heart race almost as fast as her car. After five days, he was finally going to see Joni Evans, his friend.

And he hoped she'd changed her answer to yes.

JONI KNEW she was in trouble the moment she saw Sam standing beside Marty's car.

"Look, Mom, Peter's here. He's with Sam!" Brady exclaimed, stretching as far as his seat belt would allow to see the ranch house.

Joni wanted to bury her head in the snow, close her eyes to avoid looking at him, or at least turn the car around.

She couldn't do any of those things.

"How nice," she said, trying to keep her voice from trembling.

She must not have been successful.

"Are you gonna cry?" Brady asked in concern.

"Of course not. Why would I cry?"

"I don't know, but you've been acting kind of funny lately."

How sad when she can't even hide her worries from her four-year-old. She pressed her lips firmly together, determined not to let Sam know how his intentions affected her.

She stopped the car beside Marty's and shut off the engine. Brady immediately undid his seat belt and jumped out of the car, shouting Peter's name.

While Brady moved toward Peter, Sam was coming in the opposite direction. Toward her.

She got out of the car, her knees knocking. Hunger consumed her. She'd missed him so much. Just to see him brought more joy than she'd experienced in a while.

Sam had no intention of settling for a look.

Without a word, he pulled her into his embrace, his lips covering hers, his hands pressing her against him.

Oh, boy, she was in trouble.

Chapter Sixteen

Somewhere during that kiss, that devastating, mind-blowing kiss, Joni gave up the fight.

When Sam finally lifted his mouth from hers, he growled, "The answer had better be yes."

All she could do was nod.

His lips joined hers again.

"You two ever coming in?" Loretta called from the door.

"That wouldn't be my first choice," Sam whispered in Joni's ear after he released her lips.

She closed her eyes and leaned against him. "We have to go in. They're watching us."

He lifted her face and touched foreheads with her. "Okay, but don't move more than a foot from me. I've missed you."

Without waiting for her agreement, he took her hand and led her to the house.

Loretta and Marty hugged her, but Sam didn't move away. He stood patiently, waiting for her to turn her attention back to him. She was afraid to do so.

She wasn't sure she could keep from touching him, kissing him, asking him to hold her.

"Mom, where's the cake? Didn't you bring it in?" Brady asked anxiously.

"Oh, sorry, I forgot," she replied, turning back toward the door.

"She was distracted," Marty said with a grin.

Sam glared at his sister, then turned to Joni. "I'll get it. You stay here where it's warm."

Joni watched him leave until the door closed behind him. Then, when she faced the other two women, she found them watching her with smiles on their faces. "I'm—I'm afraid he might drop it. The snow is icy today."

"He'll be careful," Loretta assured her. "It's so good to see the two of you. Did you find Sam's present at the store I suggested?"

"Yes. Uh, Brady, you and Peter should go help Sam. You can bring in all the presents we brought." She shrugged her shoulders. "I don't know why I didn't think of that."

"Like I said, you were distracted," Marty repeated, this time with a laugh.

Joni's cheeks flamed. Even if his family didn't know that Sam wasn't ready to consider marriage, she did.

When Sam and the two boys came back in, Joni rushed to take the platter of cookies from Brady. He was holding it at a precarious angle and she feared the carefully decorated cookies would splatter all over the kitchen floor.

"Look at this, Mom," Sam said, holding the Christmas cake out for his mother to see. "Joni did a great job, didn't she?"

"And Brady," Joni hurriedly added. "He did more of the decorating."

Loretta exclaimed over the cake, setting it in the center of the table. "I'm putting it here so Tom can see it before we cut it. This will be the perfect touch to Christmas dinner. You and Brady will come, won't you?"

"Oh, no, I—"

Before Joni could complete her refusal, Sam's arm went around her shoulder and he said, "They'll be here."

Brady and Peter whooped and hollered until Marty suggested they go play in the den. "Shall we make them save their presents to each other until then?"

Joni was uncomfortable. Marty and Loretta acted as if she and her son were about to become family members. But they were wrong. "I— Whatever you think."

"Sit down," Loretta urged. "I'll make us some tea. Sam, are you going to help your father work?"

Indecision, surprising in Sam, was on his face. Before he could answer, however, the boys came rushing back into the kitchen.

"Mama, can Brady come to my house? And spend the night?"

Joni started to protest, but Sam grabbed her hand and squeezed.

"I think that's a lovely idea," Marty replied with

a smile. "Would you mind, Joni? Maybe it would give you a chance to do some last-minute things, and the boys would have such fun."

"But, Marty, tomorrow is Christmas Eve. I'm sure you have lots to do."

"Not at all. Besides, I have Paul to help me. Please?"

Brady, of course, stared at his mother, on tenterhooks for permission.

Feeling the inevitability, Joni nodded. "Of course he can, if you're sure."

"I'm sure. We'll follow you back to your house and he can pack an overnight bag."

"Well, I'm going back to work. Uh, Joni, will you walk me outside?" Sam said.

His mother and sister pretended his request was normal, but Joni knew better. She didn't turn him down, however. She knew it was an excuse for him to kiss her.

As soon as they were on the porch, and the door closed, he pulled her into his arms and kissed her, his lips conveying his desires quite clearly.

When he lifted his mouth, he muttered, "I'll be there as soon as I can get away."

Then he strode off toward the barn, his hat pulled low on his forehead, determination in his every step.

JONI WAS A NERVOUS WRECK.

Brady had left with Marty and her children several hours ago. Joni had tidied the house, as if Sam would notice, and then tried to relax in a hot bubble bath.

But she couldn't.

She'd fixed a light supper, in case Sam was hungry.

She'd turned on the Christmas tree lights so the house would look festive.

She'd put on a red dress.

There was nothing left to do but pace the floor and worry. What if their lovemaking fell short of expectations? She wanted Sam so badly, yet it had been a long time since she was with a man. In fact, she'd never been with a man she wanted as much as Sam.

The sound of his truck sent panic shooting through her. What if *he* didn't want her after tonight?

He banged on the door, impatience in every knock.

Joni froze, feeling as if she were poised on a cliff, about to jump off without a parachute.

"Joni?" he called.

If she didn't answer the door, he'd alert the entire neighborhood. She crossed the room and opened it.

As if he were a whirlwind, Sam blew into the house and scooped her up into his arms. His lips settled on hers, tasting and teasing, as if he were as starved as she. She struggled to be let down, not because she wanted to escape, but because she wanted to feel him with every inch of her body.

When he finally let her breathe again, his chest heaved with his own breathing. But he didn't let her walk away. His arms held her against him.

"I—I turned on the Christmas lights," she finally whispered, unable to think of anything to say. Her gaze remained fastened on his incredible lips, longing for more kisses.

"Very festive," he agreed. Then his lips took hers once more. As if she were coming home, she fit perfectly against him, willing him to come closer with every breath. All her nervous fears had disappeared. She was where she wanted, needed to be.

He broke off the kiss and leaned his forehead against hers. "These past few days have been awful. I missed you more than I thought possible."

"Me, too." She wasn't sure of the proper etiquette in this situation. "Have you eaten? I fixed a meal."

He blinked several times, then smiled. "That would be great. I didn't take time to eat at home."

She led the way into the kitchen and quickly set the supper on the table. When she would have sat down, however, she found Sam had a different idea of dinner. He pulled her into his lap. "What are you doing?" she shrieked, taken by surprise.

"Preparing to enjoy my meal. I don't want you too far away, so we'll share a chair." He picked up a fork and speared a piece of chicken, lifting it to her mouth.

After chewing, she said, "I cooked for you, not me." She took the fork away from him and fed him a bite.

"Mmm, good. But not as tasty as this." Then he kissed her.

He was right.

They continued to feed each other occasional bites, interspersed with heated kisses. After shoving off his coat, something they'd both forgotten, Joni began unbuttoning his shirt, delighting in touching his chest.

The heated flesh and rough hairs thrilled her as she rubbed her hand across it.

"Joni," he protested.

"You don't want me to touch you?" she asked, concerned.

"Baby, I love for you to touch me, but I can't hold out much longer. And I want to do a lot of touching, too, before I lose control," he finished with a groan as she ran her fingertips over one of his nipples.

He abruptly stood, with her in his arms, and headed for the bedroom.

After several long, deep kisses when he reached her bed, he whispered, "This is a beautiful dress, Joni, but I've dreamed of seeing you without anything. Mind if we get a little more comfortable?"

Her answer was to push his shirt off his shoulders. She wanted to see him, too. She stroked his muscular chest, then slid her arms around his neck as he stood her on the floor.

"Hey, no fair," he protested, but he was grinning. He lowered the zipper on her dress and it pooled on the floor with his help.

The sudden urge to cover herself was chased away by the excitement in Sam's eyes. "Nice underwear," he teased. She'd chosen red lace to match her dress. "I like my Christmas present."

"I'm glad," she whispered. "But you're over-dressed."

He pulled his boots off. As soon as he stood, Joni reached for his belt. Between the two of them, they were naked on the bed in seconds. Joni went into Sam's arms without hesitation.

She loved this man, more than she'd ever loved anyone. She wanted nothing more than to be with him. His hands touched every part of her, memorizing her, teasing her...loving her.

And she returned the favor. His strength, his passion, his gentleness, gave her incredible pleasure. She tried to give as much back. She'd never felt so safe, so loved...or so excited in her life. His broad shoulders were her anchor and she clung to them, dropped kisses on them, as Sam loved every inch of her.

"I'm crazy about this little freckle," Sam whispered, his lips touching her just above her left breast.

"I've—I've always thought it was ugly."

He reached up to kiss her lips again. "There's nothing ugly about you, sweetheart, inside or out."

Her heart swelled. Knowing she pleased this man filled her with incredible joy. And even greater anticipation. "Sam, I can't wait any longer. Please," she urged, pulling him closer.

"Me, neither," he whispered, positioning his large body over hers.

She arched up to meet him, eager for his total possession. "Yes, Sam," she intoned. Her hands trailed down his back to his buttocks, urging him even closer.

When he entered her, it was greater than anything Joni had even imagined, much less experienced. All her earlier doubts were swept away in a flood of intense feeling. Sam's body seemed made for hers, and his every move brought her closer to fulfillment. As she stepped over the brink he joined her, and together they found the ecstasy they'd sought.

Long afterward, she held him against her, reveling in the feel of his weight atop her.

"Joni," he finally whispered, "I'm afraid I'm crushing you. Did I hurt you? Are you all right?" He slid to one side, his arms drawing her with him.

Burying her face in his neck, afraid he'd see how much she loved him, she said, "I'm fine. Better than fine. I'm— It was— I can't—"

"Me, too," he said, then kissed her again. And again.

"Oh, Sam," she moaned, stunned by her hunger for him.

"Yeah." He chuckled, she supposed at her incoherent response. Then he pulled her into his arms and began to love her again.

THE ALARM WENT OFF at four-thirty. Joni struggled to awaken, wondering why she'd wanted to get up so early. Especially when she was so snug and warm.

"I have to go, sweetheart," Sam whispered in her ear.

Reminded of the events of the night, Joni's eyes popped open. Dawn hadn't even begun, but their night of lovemaking had ended.

Sam kissed her, then shoved back the cover and got up. She stared at his hard, muscular body in the shadowy room, remembering how she'd claimed it as hers during the night. Her cheeks flushed.

He slid on his underwear and jeans, then his shirt. Sitting down on the bed, he pulled on his boots. With every article of clothing he put on, depression filled Joni.

Turning around, he leaned across the bed for one more kiss. Her arms went around his neck, wanting to hold him there, to keep reality from intruding.

But she couldn't.

"Say hello to Brady for me," he said, smiling.

She stared at him, her heart aching. She couldn't tell Brady about their night. That had been her compromise. She'd promised herself she could explore her relationship with Sam if she could keep it from hurting Brady.

"Are you all right?" he whispered, frowning at her.

"Yes, I'm fine," she assured him. She even tried to give him a smile. It wasn't a great success.

"I'll call you," he said, then added a kiss before she heard his whispered goodbye.

She lay still and silent in the bed, listening to his booted footsteps, the shutting of the front door, the sound of his truck driving away.

She hadn't even realized silent tears were coursing down her face until she lay alone in the silent house.

In the last two minutes she realized she wasn't going to be able to juggle her emotions, to stop hungering for Sam until they could steal time alone. She wasn't going to be able to hide this part of her life from her son.

She was an all-or-nothing girl.

And she'd just made the biggest mistake of her life.

SAM TUGGED on the barbed wire fence, scowling at it. He'd just spent the entire night making love to a wonderful woman. He'd never imagined sex could be so fulfilling, so exciting. Even now, he wanted her.

But something was wrong.

It wasn't the sex.

It wasn't Joni.

He yanked on the reel of barbed wire, sending it rolling until it hit a fence post. Henry looked at him questioningly, but Sam said nothing to the ranch hand. How could he explain when he didn't understand himself what was wrong.

What was wrong?

He hadn't promised her anything. She knew that. It wasn't like Dusty when he'd promised to marry Lisa.

Sam had explained to Joni that he wasn't ready to commit to anything. Not yet. But he wanted to explore their relationship. To explore Joni, he added, a smile appearing from nowhere as he remembered their night together.

Maybe after a few months...one or two...he'd be ready to make a commitment. He should at least take a little time after his divorce to be sure. He didn't want to make a mistake again.

After Henry nailed the wire to the fence post and they moved to the next one, he said, "Heard you got yourself a new lady. A real looker."

Sam's chest ached. "She's a friend."

Henry laughed. "Yeah, I heard."

Sam started to protest again, but he didn't have the stomach for it.

"Got a little boy?"

"Yeah. You've probably seen Brady around the ranch. He's a great kid."

"It's tough being a stepfather."

"Yeah." And there was part of the problem. He wanted to be Brady's stepfather, his "daddy" for Christmas. He loved the little guy.

He tried to shut out the thought that came barreling after that one. But he couldn't.

He loved Joni.

Loved her to distraction. Wanted her in his arms constantly. Wanted to show her off, brag on his lady. Instead he'd made love to her all night and snuck away before dawn.

Like a thief.

He threw himself into his work, trying to avoid his thoughts, but he couldn't. He'd said he should wait to make a new commitment. He'd said he didn't know if he'd ever want to marry again.

He was wrong.

The picture of Joni coming down the aisle toward him had his heart racing, his libido working overtime. He already knew they were perfect in bed together. Perfect? Even that word didn't come close to describing the heaven he found in her arms.

How could he deny they were perfect for each other in every other way? She was a loving, generous woman. And he wanted to claim her as his own.

"Henry, I lied."

Nailing wire to the next post, Henry looked up, surprised. "About what?"

"About Joni. I'm going to marry her."

"Congratulations. Now pull that wire a little tighter." And he went on with his work as if Sam had said the weather was good.

Sam laughed out loud, joy filling him.

ALL DAY, Joni did what she had to do, but her heart wasn't in it. She was facing a difficult decision.

She couldn't stay here in Saddle. She couldn't carry on with Sam without others finding out. And then Brady would know. She wasn't even sure why she'd thought she could.

Though she'd enjoyed every minute of their love-making, wanted it to last forever, it hadn't. It wouldn't. Sam would come to her in the dark of the night and leave as he had this morning. Hiding what they shared.

As much as she loved him, she couldn't remain in Saddle.

How she hated the thought of telling Brady.

She decided Brady deserved Christmas without that pain. But could she face going out to the ranch and looking at Sam? And did he intend to see her before Christmas Day? She had her excuses ready. Brady would be with her.

And he'd stay with her until they left the town. There would be no more long nights of loving with Sam Crawford.

She wept.

That night, she and Brady sat beside the Christmas tree, admiring the bright lights, the ornaments they'd placed on it, even the candy canes.

They were drinking hot chocolate before she tucked Brady in.

"I wish Sam were here," he said with a sigh, snuggling against his mother.

"I thought you would want Peter."

"No, I want Sam. Peter's my friend. But Sam's— Sam's like a daddy."

She hugged her son tightly against her. "We're okay, just the two of us. Don't you think?"

"Sure, Mom, but it would be nice if Sam was here."

After a painful silence, Joni said, "Sometimes we can't have what we want. I didn't want your real daddy to die, but things happen."

"Were you sad?"

"Of course I was, Brady. Your daddy and I didn't have a good marriage, but we might have worked something out. And I wouldn't wish harm to him."

"I know. I don't really remember him much, but I remember you being sad."

"You always made me feel better. You're the best son a mother could have," she told him with a smile.

He hugged her neck. "You're the best mommy, too."

He leaned against her, seemingly content. Until he asked his next question. "Does Sam make you cry?"

"Why do you ask that?"

"Today you seem sad."

"With Christmas coming?" She forced a chuckle. "I'm looking forward to opening my presents."

Her son stared at her.

And that was why she couldn't hide anything from her son. He seemed to sense her mood.

Hugging him close, she said, "Everyone in your life can do things that make you happy or sad. But it's up to you to deal with it. We're all responsible for our own happiness."

"If you tell Sam what's wrong, he'll take care of it, Mom. I know he will."

His faith in Sam was endearing, even if he was wrong.

"Sweetie, things don't always work out the way we want."

Before he could ask any more questions, questions that she couldn't answer, she said, "Time for bed, young man." She shifted him off her lap and stood up. "Santa has to come visit you."

"Mom, can Santa really bring what I asked for?"

"A train? I imagine so."

"No, not the train." He turned a troubled face to her, and she went down on her knees beside him.

"I don't know, sweetie," she whispered as she hugged him. "Just remember, Santa will do his best. If he doesn't bring you everything you asked for, it's not because he doesn't want to. Some things aren't possible."

He pulled back from her embrace. "But it's okay to hope, isn't it?"

Praying the tears in her eyes wouldn't fall, she hugged him again. "Of course, Brady. We can always hope."

SAM AND HENRY had repaired the fence line on the east end of the ranch, working in amiable silence for the last few hours. For the first time in his life Sam felt the work couldn't go fast enough. All he could think about was rushing to be with Joni, to tell her of his feelings. He closed his eyes and saw her incredible smile. Just then the wire whipped out of Sam's gloved hands and buried itself in his cheek and hand. At his outcry, Henry rushed over, pulling out his wire cutters and releasing Sam. Blood flowed from the nasty cuts.

Henry helped Sam to his horse, and they rode hard toward the ranch house. On the cell phone Henry called Tom to meet them with the truck. Sam needed medical attention.

When he balked at going to the see the doc, Tom insisted. On the ride to the clinic all Sam could think of was seeing Joni. It was as if thoughts of her shut out the pain of the cuts. He felt nothing but elation. He loved Joni Evans, and her little boy. And as soon as he could get fixed up, he was going to tell her.

It was already late afternoon. Sam had intended to go see Joni tonight, but he couldn't do anything until the doctor finished with him, particularly since his father was standing guard.

"Dad, I told Joni I'd call her. Can I at least use a phone?"

The doctor entered the cubicle at that moment, and

Tom didn't bother to answer. They gave him local anesthesia and sewed up the damage. But the painkillers they gave him afterward knocked him for a loop. He barely remembered returning to his father's truck and starting the drive home.

"We Crawfords aren't having much luck with our hands lately," Tom complained, obviously thinking of Loretta.

The word hand reminded Sam. "Dad, we gotta go by the jewelry store."

Tom stared at him. "What are you talking about? It's Christmas Eve. I'm sure the store closed hours ago."

"Call Cy and get him to open up." His words were slightly slurred, but he was determined. "He'll do it for you."

Tom slowed to a stop. "Are you sure, son?"

"Damn sure."

An hour later, with his father's help, Sam staggered from the store, satisfied with his transaction. As he sat in the truck, his purchase safe and snug in his jacket pocket, he lay his head back and relaxed for the first time all day.

And promptly passed out.

"MOM, SANTA'S HERE! Santa's here!" As Brady burst into the living room, his screams woke Joni with a start. At some point during the long, difficult night, she'd stumbled out to the couch. She couldn't lie in her bed without remembering the time spent there with Sam.

Now, with her son shaking her and pulling her arm, she slowly pushed herself up from the pillow, her head feeling groggy.

"You mean he's been here," she stated. She was glad her son was so ecstatic over his train and the other things she'd spread out beneath the tree.

"No, he's here!" Brady assured her with a giggle. "Come look."

Dread filled her stomach. She grabbed her robe, shrugged it on and followed Brady to the front door he now had standing open.

A familiar truck was parked in front of her house, with a horse trailer connected. And a tall, handsome cowboy emerged from the horse trailer, leading a buckskin colt.

"See, he's wearing a Santa coat," Brady said pointedly, giggling again.

Sure enough, Sam sported the Santa coat he'd worn their first day in Saddle. There was no padding this time, just a lean muscular body underneath. He wore his cowboy hat, not a Santa cap, and jeans and cowboy boots. But the boots were black.

And he was leading the colt up to the front door.

Great. He'd not only broken her heart, but he was also determined to break Brady's, too.

Anger surged through her.

"Brady, go get dressed, and don't come outside until I say you can."

"But, Mom—" her son protested.

"Do as I say, Brady," she said sternly, fighting back the tears.

"Okay, Mom," Brady whispered. Gone was the happy little boy who had awakened.

She felt like a monster.

And someone was going to pay.

As soon as Brady headed to his room, she stepped out on the front porch, pulling the door behind her.

"What do you think you're doing?" she asked in an angry voice.

"Playing Santa," Sam said, a big smile on his face.

"Take that animal and get out of here."

"But, Joni—"

"I told you you couldn't give that horse to Brady," she suddenly wailed, losing her self-control. "You've ruined Christmas for him!"

Sam stared at her, as if she'd lost her mind. Maybe she had. She'd certainly lost her heart.

"You said only a parent could give a present like Cookie."

"So?" What was wrong with the man? If he didn't leave soon, she was going to embarrass herself.

"Well, I figure I've got the right, then."

Joni didn't know what to say. She was afraid to hope, even though she'd told Brady last night it was okay.

Sam tied the colt to the porch railing, then stepped up to Joni's level. "I want to be Brady's daddy for Christmas."

Joni stared at him, unable to speak.

"And most of all, I want to love his mommy—for the rest of our lives. I don't intend to sneak out before dawn ever again. I want to tell everyone you're mine." He cupped her face with his hands. "Joni, will you marry me?"

"But—but you said you weren't ready."

"I was wrong. I can't wait. I don't want to lose you."

"But I didn't tell anyone we were leaving," she said, unable to think.

"You were leaving?" Sam didn't wait any longer for her answer. He swept her into his arms and kissed the breath out of her.

When he let her go, she asked the question she'd gotten sidetracked from earlier. "Sam, what happened to your face?"

He grinned. "That's why we have to get married. You distract me too much."

"You hurt yourself because of me?" she demanded, anguish in her voice.

"Hey, sweetheart, I'm okay. I got careless with some barbed wire. But I'm patched up. I couldn't come last night so I wanted to get here before Brady woke up this morning."

"Too late. He's already up."

"You are going to marry me, aren't you?"

She loved the worry in his voice. She wanted to marry him with all her heart, but only if that's what he wanted. "Are you sure?"

"So sure I got this last night." He pulled a box from his pocket and popped open the lid. Joni stared at a perfect diamond ring. He took it out of the box and put it on her finger. "If you don't like it, we can exchange it. But not till tomorrow. I already bothered Cyrus enough last night.''

She threw her arms around his neck. "Oh, Sam, it's beautiful. I love it.'' She didn't bother to wipe the tears that welled in her eyes and spilled down her cheeks.

Sam did, and then he kissed her.

"Can I come out now, Mom?'' Brady whispered from the door.

Sam released Joni and looked over her shoulder. "Sure you can, Brady. Come see what Santa brought you.''

Joni nodded to her son, reinforcing Sam's invitation.

"Do you mean it, Sam? Do I get to have Cookie?''

"You do, son. He's your very own horse.''

Brady flew down the steps, his arms encircling the colt's neck. "Wow! I never thought—I mean, Santa brought me almost everything I asked for.''

"I think Santa can do better than that. He's a pretty special guy, you know. What else did you want?'' Sam squatted down to Brady's level.

After shifting his gaze from Sam to his mother and then back again, Brady ducked his head. "I—I wanted a daddy.''

"Will I do?'' Sam asked softly.

Again, Brady looked at his mother. When he saw her nod, he leaped toward Sam, his arms going around the cowboy's neck. "Really? Really? Are you sure? You mean I could be your real little boy?''

"My real little boy,'' Sam agreed, hugging him

back. With a silent prayer of thanks and with Brady in his arms, he reached out for Joni. "My real family. My real love."

He was grateful he'd been given a second chance for love, for family. He couldn't ask for a better son than Brady. And a better wife than Joni.

Playing Santa was the smartest thing he'd ever done.

Epilogue

Christmas Eve.

Sam leaned against his pitchfork, grinning. It had been a year since Joni and Brady had come into his life. They had a lot to celebrate.

"Dad?"

He turned to the sturdy five-year-old who had just walked into the barn. "Yeah, son? Everything okay at the house?"

"Sure."

Sam studied the boy. Lately, it seemed something had been bothering Brady, but he hadn't said anything.

"You sure?"

Brady dragged his booted toe in the straw. Then he said, "What if I changed my mind?"

"About what?"

"About the baby. I don't want it anymore."

Sam drew a deep breath. He and Joni—and Brady—were expecting a new addition to their family any day. It was a little late to have a change of heart. "Why is that, son?" he asked.

Brady climbed on the railing and stared at the mare in the stall. "'Cause Mom is tired all the time. And she didn't even go cut down the Christmas tree with us."

"She will next year. All that bouncing in the truck wouldn't be good for her right now."

"What if—what if you love this baby more than me?" Brady finally asked in a low voice.

"Whatever gave you that idea?"

"Peter said this baby would be part you," Brady said, still staring at the horse. "I'm not."

Sam put aside his pitchfork and plucked the child off the railing into his arms. "Yes, you are."

"Peter said—"

"Peter doesn't know. You see, you're part of my heart, like your mom. You believe I love your mom, don't you?"

Brady nodded.

"I got to choose you and your mom, and I love you both with all my heart. Love isn't limited, son. The more you give, the more there is to give. And you know what?"

Brady, his gaze more hopeful, slung his arm around Sam's neck. "What?"

"This baby will be my second son. You'll always be my first son."

"We're having a boy?" Brady asked, excitement in his voice.

Sam and Joni had known the sex of their baby, but they'd kept it secret from the rest of the family. "Yes, we are," Sam told him, hoping Joni would forgive him for breaking his word.

"Wow! I thought it would be an old girl."

"We'll try for a girl next time." Sam assured him with a chuckle. "But this little boy is going to need his big brother to show him everything. Think you'll be up to the job?"

"Yeah, sure. I'll even let him ride Cookie. When he's older. Just for a little while till he gets his own horse."

"So you don't want to take back your request to Santa?"

"Naw. Besides, Santa does a pretty good job. I got you, didn't I?" Brady said with a laugh.

"You sure did. And that same Santa is going to give you a little brother."

The cell phone he carried with him at all times now, even to the barn, rang. Sam's eyes widened. Lowering Brady to the barn floor, he grabbed the phone.

"Yeah?"

"Sam, I think it's time."

"Santa's on his way," Sam assured Joni and scooped up Brady, then raced to the house.

It was time for another Santa delivery.

Take 2 bestselling love stories FREE

Plus get a FREE surprise gift!

Special Limited-Time Offer

Mail to Harlequin Reader Service®

3010 Walden Avenue
P.O. Box 1867
Buffalo, N.Y. 14240-1867

YES! Please send me 2 free Harlequin American Romance® novels and my free surprise gift. Then send me 4 brand-new novels every month, which I will receive months before they appear in bookstores. Bill me at the low price of $3.34 each plus 25¢ delivery and applicable sales tax, if any.* That's the complete price, and a saving of over 10% off the cover prices—quite a bargain! I understand that accepting the books and gift places me under no obligation ever to buy any books. I can always return a shipment and cancel at any time. Even if I never buy another book from Harlequin, the 2 free books and the surprise gift are mine to keep forever.

154 HEN CH7E

Name	(PLEASE PRINT)	
Address	Apt. No.	
City	State	Zip

This offer is limited to one order per household and not valid to present Harlequin American Romance® subscribers. *Terms and prices are subject to change without notice. Sales tax applicable in N.Y.

UAMER-98

©1990 Harlequin Enterprises Limited

Christmas Is For Kids

This Christmas, some of your favorite
Harlequin American Romance authors bring
you brand-new stories that will warm your heart!
In December 1998, don't miss:

#753 SMOOCHIN' SANTA
by Jule McBride

#754 BABY'S FIRST CHRISTMAS
by Cathy Gillen Thacker

#755 COWBOY SANTA
by Judy Christenberry

#756 GIFT-WRAPPED DAD
by Muriel Jensen

Available at your favorite retail outlet.

Fill your holiday with...
excitement, magic and love!

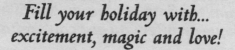

December is the time for Christmas carols, surprises
wrapped in colored paper and kisses under the mistletoe.
Mistletoe Kisses is a festive collection of stories about three
humbug bachelors and the feisty heroines who entice them
to ring in the holiday season with love and kisses.

AN OFFICER AND A GENTLEMAN
by Rachel Lee

THE MAGIC OF CHRISTMAS
by Andrea Edwards

THE PENDRAGON VIRUS
by Cait London

Available December 1998
wherever Harlequin and Silhouette books are sold.

HARLEQUIN®
Makes any time special ™

Silhouette®

***For a limited time, Harlequin and Silhouette
have an offer you just can't refuse.***

In November and December 1998:

BUY **ANY** TWO HARLEQUIN
OR SILHOUETTE BOOKS and
SAVE $10.00
off future purchases

OR BUY ANY THREE HARLEQUIN OR SILHOUETTE BOOKS
AND **SAVE $20.00** OFF FUTURE PURCHASES!

(each coupon is good for $1.00 off the purchase of two
Harlequin or Silhouette books)

···

JUST BUY 2 HARLEQUIN OR SILHOUETTE BOOKS, SEND US YOUR
NAME, ADDRESS AND 2 PROOFS OF PURCHASE (CASH REGISTER
RECEIPTS) AND HARLEQUIN WILL SEND YOU A COUPON BOOKLET
WORTH $10.00 OFF FUTURE PURCHASES OF HARLEQUIN OR
SILHOUETTE BOOKS IN 1999. SEND US 3 PROOFS OF PURCHASE AND
WE WILL SEND YOU 2 COUPON BOOKLETS WITH A TOTAL SAVING OF
$20.00. (ALLOW 4-6 WEEKS DELIVERY) OFFER EXPIRES
DECEMBER 31, 1998.

···

I accept your offer! Please send me a coupon booklet(s), to:

NAME: _____

ADDRESS: _____

CITY: _____ STATE/PROV.: _____ POSTAL/ZIP CODE: _____

Send your name and address, along with your cash register
receipts for proofs of purchase, to:

In the U.S.	In Canada
Harlequin Books	Harlequin Books
P.O. Box 9057	P.O. Box 622
Buffalo, NY	Fort Erie, Ontario
14269	L2A 5X3

PHQ4982

HARLEQUIN®

A M E R I C A N ◆ R O M A N C E ®

COMING NEXT MONTH

#757 SANTA SLEPT OVER by Jule McBride
The Little Matchmaker
Christmas morning…on the trail of their missing mischievous
matchmaking daughter…in a swirling snowstorm…how did Joy and
Ryan Holt wake up in an inn bedroom—together, smiling and wearing
only a Santa hat?

#758 DADDY'S LITTLE DARLINGS by Tina Leonard
Gowns of White
When Alexander Banning learned his estranged—darn stubborn—
wife was pregnant, he set out to win back her love—and his male heir of
his Texas family ranch. But Daphne didn't make either easy for the
determined daddy. Not only did she deliver triplets, but they came
wrapped in ruffles, white lace and satin!

#759 THE COWBOY IS A DADDY by Mindy Neff
When Wyoming cowboy Brice DeWitt placed an ad for a housekeeper-
cook at his Flying D Ranch, he expected a sturdy, mature woman—not
a petite, pregnant applicant who was about to deliver on his doorstep!

#760 RICH, SINGLE & SEXY by Mary Anne Wilson
The Ultimate…
With a seductive smile and knockout kisses, Connor McKay truly was
"The Ultimate Catch." But this sexy billionaire aimed to keep his
bachelor status. Then he met Maggie Palmer.…

Look us up on-line at: http://www.romance.net